A Love Redeemed

Lisa Jordan

LOVE INSPIRED
INSPIRATIONAL ROMANCE

LOVE INSPIRED®
INSPIRATIONAL ROMANCE

Recycling programs
for this product may
not exist in your area.

ISBN-13: 978-1-335-48840-4

A Love Redeemed

Copyright © 2020 by Lisa Jordan

This edition published by arrangement with Harlequin Books S.A.

For questions and comments about the quality of this book,
please contact us at CustomerService@Harlequin.com.

Love Inspired
22 Adelaide St. West, 40th Floor
Toronto, Ontario M5H 4E3, Canada
www.Harlequin.com

Printed in U.S.A.

"Are you going to be our new mommy?"

Isabella gave little Olivia a startled look. "What? No. Why do you ask that?"

"Because you and my daddy are holding hands."

Isabella dropped Tucker's hand as if it were on fire and clasped hers behind her back.

Tucker laughed, a warm, rich sound that flowed through Isabella. "Let's take Isabella down to visit the farm."

Tucker ushered them out the door and into the afternoon sunshine. The twins ran ahead, but Olivia stopped to pick some purple flowers growing alongside the road, then held them out to Isabella.

"Thank you. Purple's my favorite color."

"Mine, too."

Maybe Isabella didn't need to be Mary Poppins or have a degree in early childhood education. After all, she could totally relate to the young motherless child on so many levels. And perhaps that was the key to building this relationship.

Hope bloomed in her chest, filling her with excitement for the first time since agreeing to Tucker's suggestion. After all, it was for only a couple of weeks. She could handle it for Tucker's sake…and for her own.

Lisa Jordan has been writing for over a decade, taking a hiatus to earn her degree in early childhood education. By day, she operates an in-home family childcare business. By night, she writes contemporary Christian romances. Being a wife to her real-life hero and mother to two young-adult men overflows her cup of blessings. In her spare time, she loves reading, knitting and hanging out with family and friends. Learn more about her at lisajordanbooks.com.

Books by Lisa Jordan

Love Inspired

Lakeside Reunion
Lakeside Family
Lakeside Sweethearts
Lakeside Redemption
Lakeside Romance
Season of Hope
A Love Redeemed

Visit the Author Profile page at Harlequin.com.

For I know the thoughts that I think toward you,
saith the Lord, thoughts of peace,
and not of evil, to give you an expected end.
Then shall ye call upon me, and ye shall go
and pray unto me, and I will hearken unto you.
And ye shall seek me, and find me, when
ye shall search for me with all your heart.
—*Jeremiah* 29:11–13

Thank You, Lord, for this writing dream and walking with me daily to make it happen.

Acknowledgments

Susan May Warren—thank you for answering the call of the pineapple. Without you, this book wouldn't have been written.

To my son Scott Jordan, whose culinary talents bless me. Thank you for helping me to create Isabella and adding authenticity to this story. Pieces of your heart are in her. I love you forever.

Jeanne Takenaka—thank you for being my walking buddy.

Bill Nobles, Doug and Dalyn Weller, Christy Miller, Jeanne Takenaka— thank you for helping with research. I appreciate your time. Any mistakes are mine.

My MBT Core team, WiWee sisters, Joy Seekers Huddle, Coffee Girls, Cyber Sisters, WWC family—your prayers and encouragement keep me going…and growing. I love you all.

My family—Patrick, Mitchell, Scott, Sarah and Bridget. You are my reasons for reaching for my dreams. I love you forever.

Rachelle Gardner and Melissa Endlich— thank you for continually encouraging and inspiring me to grow as a writer. So thankful you're on my team.

The Love Inspired team who works hard to bring my books to print.

Chapter One

For the first time in forty-eight hours, Isabella could breathe.

She was home safely, and everything would be okay now. Even if she didn't know what that looked like just yet.

All she wanted was to crawl into her childhood bed and pull the covers over her head until the humiliation of the last forty-eight hours was nothing more than a distant memory.

Driving from upstate New York to Shelby Lake in northwestern Pennsylvania with heavy mid-October rain pelting the windshield while getting boxed in by semis as she tried to stay in her lane had turned her into a jumble of nerves.

Stay in her lane.

Advice she should've taken to avoid tanking her career.

She should've known better than to take such a risk at the upscale resort where she worked as a saucier. But when their head pastry chef was hospitalized for emergency surgery, she wanted to prove to Justin Wilkes, her boss, she could handle making the wedding desserts at the last minute.

With her own shellfish allergy, she knew how vital food safety was and took every precaution against cross-contamination. The pastry kitchen had been spotless before she started baking. So how did a bridesmaid end up in anaphylactic shock from peanut exposure?

Maybe Justin was right—maybe she was nothing more than a greasy spoon girl.

No, she refused to believe God would give her this dream only to take it away. But, man, losing her job sure felt like it.

Kicking off her damp flip-flops, she changed out of her wet jeans and T-shirt into gray flannel pajama pants and a long-sleeved light blue T-shirt. She pulled back the comforter and crawled into the bed that had been hers from childhood until she'd graduated culinary school and left Shelby Lake nearly ten years ago to chase her dream of running her own kitchen someday.

After this week, though, she'd be fortunate to wrap burgers in some fast-food joint.

But she'd worry about that tomorrow.

Tonight, she needed sleep.

The storm continued to rage, pounding on the roof of the second-floor apartment over Joe's All-Star Diner, owned by her father. Thunder rumbled and lightning slashed, flashing brightness across the room, highlighting the white bookcase filled with yearbooks, novels with creased spines and rows of cookbooks, including the Solange Boucher collection she'd kept tucked behind the others to avoid causing her father further pain. Across the room was the matching desk with framed photos of Isabella and her father at graduation and another of Isabella and Tucker Holland when they had worked together at the diner while in high school and won the junior cook-off at the county fair.

Tucker Holland.

Wow.

Now there was a blast from the past.

Another regret to add to her list. Too afraid to make a move, she'd lost her friend to the woman he ended up marrying.

And Isabella was placed firmly in the friend zone.

She moved her pillow into a more comfortable position and pulled the comforter over her head.

From the matching nightstand, her phone played a popular TV theme song.

Without turning on the light, she reached for it, catching her former roommate's name on the display. "Hey, Jeanne."

"Girl, it's about time. Are you okay? I've been texting and calling, but I kept getting your voice mail. Where are you?"

She winced at her friend's panicked voice rising with each syllable and pulled the phone away from her ear. "Home."

"No, you're not. I'm at the apartment, and you're not here."

Isabella could picture her petite friend pacing the small five-room apartment they'd shared near the up-scale resort where they'd worked together for the past five years.

"Home as in Shelby Lake."

"What? Why? What about work?"

"Justin fired me, remember? After I ruined the Warner wedding." Tears pricked the backs of her eyes as she recalled being summoned into his office, hearing the door close with a resounding click that made her stomach bottom out, then being told she was no longer employed at the Briarwood Resort.

She'd never forget the humiliation of having to gather her knife case and personal belongings from her locker while the rest of the kitchen staff watched with pitying looks.

"Oh, Bella. Justin was a jerk for caving to management pressure. It wasn't your fault. In fact, we learned one of the busboys knocked over the peanut flour and tried to clean it up without anyone finding out. It blended in so well with the powdered sugar dusted over those gorgeous raspberry tartlets that he figured no one was the wiser. It was not your fault."

"Yet I'm the one who got fired." She closed her eyes against another surge of wetness. "I'm sorry to leave you in a lurch, Jeanne. I left a note and money for next month's rent on your dresser. I just couldn't stay."

"So, what are you going to do now?"

"Sleep, then drown my sorrows in a plate of Dad's nachos and try to figure out the rest of my life."

"How about if you slow down, skip the carbs and just focus on the next thing?"

"Great advice. You should be a life coach."

"Girl, I'm serious. You're one of the best chefs I know. You've been working hard for ten years, so walking away now is not an option. Since you've always wanted to open your own kitchen, maybe now's the time to put your plan in place."

An alarm screamed, startling Isabella and jerking her upright. "I gotta go."

After ending the call and with her heart pounding in her ears, she scrambled out of bed and flew out of the room to find bloated clouds of gray smoke rising up the stairs.

She rushed to the closed door next to hers and pounded on it. "Dad! Wake up!"

Hearing no response, she threw open the door, flicked on the light and found the bed still made and the room empty.

When she'd arrived at the diner about half an hour ago—just before midnight—all the lights had been off, and she'd parked next to Dad's fifteen-year-old pickup in the back lot. She'd assumed he was in bed, since she hadn't told him she was coming home.

Pulling her T-shirt over her nose, she raced down the stairs, eyes stinging and lungs burning. The shrieking nearly deafened her as she pushed through the swinging door to the kitchen darkened with smoke.

Jets from the fire-suppression system sprayed chemical agent across the flaming char grill, the flat top and the fryers, covering the appliances in a mucky foam blanket.

She dropped her phone on the reach-in and covered her face with shaking hands. The acrid scent of the smoke clawed at her throat, causing her to cough.

She grabbed a towel off the stainless-steel counter and dried the tears streaming down her face.

Why was Dad cooking so late?

"Dad?" Her watering eyes blurred as she moved through the kitchen calling his name.

Her bare toes stubbed against something hard, and she nearly stumbled. She grabbed the salad reach-in to keep her balance and looked down. Stifling a scream, she dropped to her knees next to her father, who was sprawled on the slip-resistant tile floor between the grill and the upright cooler, a metal spatula on the floor beside him.

"Dad!" Isabella pressed two fingers to his neck, checking for a pulse. She nearly wept at the shallow beats at his clammy throat.

She shook his shoulder. "Dad, Dad. Wake up. Can you hear me?"

Lowering her cheek above his nose and mouth, his faint breath warmed her skin. Isabella grabbed her phone off the reach-in and tapped 911.

A female voice answered. "Shelby Lake 911. What is the location of your emergency?"

"Joe's Diner. Ten thirty-one Copen Street at the bottom of Holland Hill."

"What's your name?"

"Isabella Bradley."

"What's your emergency?"

"My father's unconscious, but he's breathing and has a weak pulse. He's pale and his skin's clammy."

"Where is he now?"

"Passed out on the kitchen floor."

"Does your father have any health issues?"

"Type 2 diabetes."

"Age?"

"Fifty-five."

"I'm dispatching help. Please stay on the line."

She waited for what felt like an eternity. Within minutes, wailing sounded down the quiet street and grew louder as the ambulance pulled into the parking lot, the revolving red lights reflecting through the wet windows.

Jumping to a standing position, Isabella left her father's side long enough to unlock the rear kitchen door and throw on the lights.

Two paramedics dressed in navy windbreakers and black cargo pants rushed in out of the rain carrying medical bags. The shorter one, a woman with blond hair that brushed her shoulders, looked at Isabella with compassionate hazel eyes. "I'm Dalyn Nobles with Shelby Lake EMS."

The taller one touched her elbow. "Hey, Bella."

The deep timbre of his voice roused tucked-away memories. She looked into familiar summer sky–blue eyes—always cool and collected—inches from hers above a strong jaw and a half smile that sent her heart out of rhythm.

"Tucker." His name slipped past her lips almost like a sigh.

He wrapped her in a quick one-armed hug, then lifted his nose. "Was there a fire?"

"Dad must've been cooking and passed out. The fire suppression system put out the char grill fire."

With Dalyn beside him, Tucker hurried to her father's side and shook his shoulder. "Hey, Joe. It's Tucker. Can you hear me?"

At no response, he glanced at Isabella as he pulled out a stethoscope and listened to her father's chest. "How long has he been unconscious?"

"I don't know. I got in less than an hour ago and headed to my room. Then I heard the alarm and rushed down to the kitchen to find dispensed foam all over the cooking equipment."

"Joe was already passed out?" Tucker pulled a penlight from his pocket and shined it into her father's eyes.

"Yes." She relayed the information she'd given to the dispatcher, including his recent diabetes diagnosis.

Dalyn pulled out a small glucose meter and inserted a test strip. Then she pricked one of Dad's fingers with a lancet and squeezed a drop of blood onto the test strip. She showed the display to Tucker.

Tucker's jaw tightened. "Your dad's blood sugar is dangerously low. We need to get him to the hospital and get it stabilized." He turned to Dalyn. "Establish IV access and administer D50."

"What's D50?"

"Dextrose. It will help boost his blood sugar level." He pushed to his feet and gave Isabella's shoulder a gentle squeeze.

As the adrenaline drained from her body, she started shaking. She tucked her chin to her chest so he wouldn't see the tears that filled her eyes and shivered as a rain-soaked wind blew through the open kitchen door.

Tucker shrugged out of his jacket and draped it around her shoulders. "I'm going to grab the stretcher. You can ride in the ambulance with your dad."

Isabella glanced down at her rumpled clothes and bare feet. "I need shoes."

Casting a quick glance at her father, she headed for the doors then turned to Tucker. "Is Dad going to be okay?"

"We'll do whatever we can to make sure he is. His blood sugar had to be dangerously low for him to pass out. His brain can go only so long before permanent damage occurs."

The compassion in his eyes and his gentle smile should have soothed her, but his last words tangled around the fear settling in her stomach. "How could this happen?"

"Poor diet, lack of exercise, missing doses of meds, stress. And after he let it slip about the possibility of the diner closing, Joe's definitely been under a lot of stress."

Her hand pressed to the door, Isabella froze, her eyes wide. "Wait. W-what do you mean about the diner closing?"

Tucker looked at her, then shook his head. "Joe didn't tell you."

"No."

He scrubbed a hand over his face. "Man, Bella. I'm sorry. I assumed that's why you'd come home."

"No, I came home because…well, that doesn't matter right now." She waved away the rest of her words. "What happened?"

Tucker held up a hand. "I said too much already. We need to get him loaded into the ambulance. Talk to Joe once he's stable."

The knot in Isabella's stomach cinched tighter. The diner had been Dad's lifeline since he was left to raise a preschooler on his own, the staff and customers becoming his extended family. And that's what had given her comfort to leave for culinary school.

But the diner has always been her home away from home. Her safe place, her sense of security.

And she'd do whatever it took to preserve that.

Whatever was going on, Dad didn't have to handle it alone anymore. She'd put her own dreams on hold to help him get well again and prevent the diner from closing.

Somehow.

It had been the kind of night where someone could have died.

And if Isabella Bradley had shown up any later, then she would've had to start planning her father's funeral.

Tucker hated storms, particularly tornados, but last night's downpour was a close second.

Especially when they had returned to the station and changed into dry uniforms, only to be called out again for a motor vehicle accident—a rollover with fatalities this time.

He and Dalyn had transported Joe Bradley to the emergency department, and as much as he'd wanted to sit with Bella until Joe was stabilized, they had returned to the station only to be called out again. Not the way he wanted to end his twenty-four-hour shift.

Pulling the bloody young man off his barely breathing

wife, who didn't survive the trip to the ER, despite being less than ten minutes away…yeah, it was getting old.

The dude's sobbing echoed Tucker's grief after losing his own wife nearly three years ago.

The kid's life wouldn't be the same again. He'd have to learn how to wake up and face the day by himself. Grief would be his new companion, coloring his world in shades of gray and despair.

No matter how many calls Tucker responded to, it never got easier. And last night's events churned up a storm within him—the unsettled feeling that change was inevitable.

Because if Tucker didn't make some changes soon, he was going to be out of a job. Then he and his five-year-old twins were going to be in a bigger mess than they were now.

In the two months since they'd moved out of the farm-house—to give his newly wedded father and stepmother the privacy they deserved—and back to the house Tucker had shared with his late wife so his twins could get set-tled before school started six weeks ago, he'd been hit with one disaster after another. That included hiring and firing two nannies before finding Mandy, who was the perfect fit for his family.

With his operations supervisor's veiled warning—or "a bit of advice," as he called it—ringing in his ears, Tucker pulled into the driveway, gravel crunching be-neath the tires of his silver SUV.

Dragging himself out from behind the wheel, he trudged to the back door, his eyes gritty and fatigue pressing down his shoulders. Inside the laundry room, Tucker unlaced his muddy boots and toed them off. Meno, his sister-in-law's goldendoodle, appeared at his side, his tail wagging and tongue ready to lick his face.

"Hey, boy." Wrapping his arms around his neck, he brushed his cheek against the dog's silky fur and closed his eyes for a second. Any longer than that and he'd fall asleep sitting up.

All he wanted was a hot shower and to crash, but that wasn't going to happen. Not with an exam to study for, a paper to finish and three chapters to read.

What made him think he could handle college classes to become a grief counselor with a demanding job and raising five-year-old children on his own?

Because he wanted to help others who were grieving to find hope.

A glance at his watch showed he had about ten minutes to see the twins before they needed to be walked to the end of the driveway, where their bus would pick them up. Then he could crash for a few hours before diving into homework.

When was the last time he'd gotten a full eight hours of sleep?

These days he'd be happy with five or six.

Hence Franco's warning of burning his candle at both ends.

He stepped into the kitchen. Leaning a shoulder and his head against the doorjamb, he sighed.

An opened box of Cheerios had been tipped over and spilled onto the floor with an open milk jug next to it. A stool sat next to the sink, and the cabinet door above the counter hung open. A small stream of water trickled into the sink, splashing over last night's dinner dishes that hadn't been loaded into the dishwasher.

Tucker scrubbed a hand over his face and pushed away from the doorway. He followed the sounds of laughter and music into the living room and found Landon still in pajamas sitting on the couch eating cheese balls from an oversize plastic barrel and his eyes glued to the TV.

"Hey, Lando, planning to go to school today?"

His eyes not leaving the cartoon, Tucker's son wiped his orange-stained hand across the front of his shirt and shrugged. Meno munched on cheese balls that had fallen on the floor.

Tucker grabbed the remote and flicked off the TV. He pulled the plastic barrel of cheese balls out of Landon's arms and snapped the blue plastic lid on top.

"Dad, I was watching that and eating those." Landon reached for the cheese balls.

Tucker held up the container. "This, my man, is not breakfast. Where's Mandy? And your sister?"

"Mandy's crying in the bathroom." Landon imitated with exaggerated sobbing noises, then laughed. "I couldn't hear my show, so I closed the door. Livie's acting like a baby."

"Why's Livie crying?"

He shrugged, then rolled his eyes. "Dunno. She cries at everything. Why are girls so 'motional all the time?"

Tucker bit back a smile and gestured to the heap of couch pillows piled on the floor. "How about if you put these pillows back where they belong and pick up your toys? Then you can head to your room and get dressed for school."

"I can't, Dad."

"Why not?"

"The pillows protect me from the burning lava."

"Landon…" His tone left no room for argument.

"Fine, but don't blame me if my feet burn up and fall off." Landon picked up the first pillow and rammed it onto the couch, pushing at it with his stomach.

"Let's risk it, okay?"

With one fire put out, Tucker left the living room, set the cheese balls on the kitchen table and then headed down the hall to find Olivia burritoed in her fleece cupcake-printed blanket in front of the bathroom door. He knelt beside her and brushed tangled blond hair out of her face. "Hey, princess."

Spying him, Olivia launched herself into his arms, tripping over her blanket as fresh sobs shook her tiny shoulders. "Daddy, I'm so glad you're home."

"What's up with the waterworks?" He sat on the floor and pulled her into his lap.

"Dad-d-dy, is Mandy leaving us?" Hiccups punctuated her words.

"Leaving? Why would you think that?"

"She said."

Ice slid through his veins. Tucker closed his eyes and pressed his forehead to hers. He couldn't afford to lose another nanny. Not now. "How about I check on Mandy? I'm sure everything's going to be okay."

"You p-promis-se?"

As he peered into her sweet face that looked so much like her mother's, it made his heart ache. He wanted to promise and wipe away the tears from her wide blue eyes. But life, especially the last few years, had taught him not to make promises he couldn't keep. "How about you get dressed, then I'll drive you and Landon to school?"

Livie covered her mouth and giggled. "Silly Daddy. There's no school today."

"What do you mean, there's no school?"

"It's parent-teacher day, remember? Mrs. Saar said she's 'cited to meet my daddy."

Tucker groaned and buried his face in his daughter's shoulder. So now in addition to having a trashed house and school assignments due, he had kids home all day and needed to work around two separate conferences for them.

So much for getting any sleep today.

With Livie still in his arms, Tucker pushed to his feet and carried her down the hall to her room. He opened the door and set her on the unmade bed. "Get dressed while I check on Mandy, okay?"

She nodded, but instead of moving toward her closet, she picked up one of her many stuffed animals and burrowed beneath the covers. Tucker cast a long look at her pillow and forced himself to leave the room. He headed back to the bathroom and knocked quietly on the door. "Mandy, is everything okay?"

The bathroom door opened, and he saw his twenty-three-year-old nanny sitting on the beige bath mat with her back pressed against the tub. Dressed in an oversize red T-shirt and navy running shorts, Mandy pulled her knees to her chest and wiped her watery eyes with a soggy tissue.

Tucker opened the linen closet and reached for the only washcloth on the shelf, trying to ignore the overflowing laundry hamper, and ran it under warm water. He wrung it out, then handed it to her.

She took it and covered her face. Sighing deeply, she shook her head. "I'm sorry, Tucker, but I can't do this anymore."

Despite being muffled by the wet cloth, her words arrowed his gut.

Tucker leaned a shoulder against the door frame and shoved his hands in his front pockets. "Do what, exactly?"

She dragged her fingers through her short dark hair and sighed. "As much as I love Landon and Olivia…and working for you, I need to give you my notice—effective immediately."

His fingers tightened into fists, and he schooled his voice to keep the welling panic from spilling all over the bathroom. "What's going on?"

"Sean broke off our engagement last night." Fresh sobs racked her shoulders. Once the tears subsided, she pulled the cloth off her face, and the hurt around the frayed edges of her voice made his chest ache for her. "I'm moving back home."

"I'm so sorry. That really stinks. Sean's the one missing out." He released a sigh. "Is there anything I can do to get you to reconsider? More money?"

She looked at him with large, watering eyes and shook her head. "I'm sorry. You deserve better than this, but I just can't stay in Shelby Lake. Every place I go reminds me of him."

He understood all too well.

She pushed to her feet. Her dark-circled eyes indicated she'd slept very little last night. "I'm really sorry. My parents are flying in tonight, helping me to pack up my apartment, then we're driving home to North Carolina." She twisted the wet rag between her fingers. "Is it okay if I say goodbye to the twins?"

He nodded, not trusting his voice.

She pushed past him, and he leaned against the sink, cradling his head in his hands.

What was he going to do now?

Sure, he could ask Dad and Claudia to help out, but that was a short-term solution to a long-term situation.

Man, he missed his wife.

Scraping his hand over his face, he caught sight of his bare ring finger, which still bore a fading tan line. Removing his wedding ring a few months ago had resulted in nothing more than leaving his hand naked and exposed, even nearly three years after Rayne's unexpected death.

He missed being married, but truth was, he'd had his happily-ever-after already.

Sure, some people like his dad and Claudia found love again.

But Tucker was a package deal. Not many women wanted a ready-made family.

Besides, how could another woman compare to what he'd had with Rayne?

With the anniversary of his late wife's death approaching, Tucker wanted more. Problem was, he wasn't quite sure what that looked like, but he was definitely ready for a bit of sunshine to brighten his days.

However, striving for a better future was taking its toll, mentally and physically. He longed for a helpmate, a life partner who would support him and not give up on him.

Someday.

Maybe.

When he was ready to risk his heart again.

He knew how messy life could be. Sure, they'd all have days of spilled cereal and cheese balls for breakfast. But after hiring Mandy to nanny his children, Tucker had had a glimpse of hope for some sort of new normal, and he didn't want to lose that.

But now he was back to square one and needed to find someone else he could trust with his children.

And that was a very short list.

Otherwise, his boss's veiled warning would result into a termination, and his family couldn't afford that. He needed his job until he finished his degree in grief counseling.

In the meantime, though, he needed to keep trusting God because something would work out.

It had to.

Chapter Two

Somehow Isabella had to get her father to listen to reason.

She laced her fingers around the coffee cup, hopefully hiding the trembling, and looked at Dad, who seemed to have aged overnight. "You're doing too much. You just got home and should be resting, especially since your doctor wanted you to stay another day."

"Why? So they can bleed more money from me? No, thanks. I feel fine. Besides, I don't have time to be lying around. I have a business to run."

Home from the hospital less than an hour, and he already had a stained apron stretched over his protruding belly while he washed vegetables at the prep sink.

His dark hair, cut to military precision, contained even more silver than when she'd been home a few months ago. His brown eyes had lost their sparkle. Laugh lines deepened into crevices of worry as he worked.

His favorite country station played softly from the black AM/FM radio sitting on a corner shelf, filling the frustrating silence.

Dad dried his hands on a paper towel, then balled it up and pitched it in the oversize black trash can. He looked at her with vacant eyes that cut through her. "I'm sorry, Bells. The last thing I wanted was for you to see your old man as a failure."

Isabella set her cup down, moved behind him and wrapped her arms around his waist, resting her cheek against his back. "You have never been nor will you ever be a failure in my eyes. You should have told me the diner was struggling. I would've helped in any way I could."

"You have your own life to lead. Besides, Tuck had no business saying anything. This is my mess. I'll handle it." He turned and patted her cheek with a wet, beefy hand.

"What happened to you and me being in this together?" Isabella crossed her arms over her chest. "This place has been paid off for years. Not to mention it's packed every day, so why are you in danger of losing everything you've built up for the last twenty-five years?"

Dad scrubbed a hand over his tired face, then shielded his eyes, but not before she caught the sheen of wetness. He cleared his throat. "I told you already—this isn't your problem."

"I'm your daughter. We've been through everything together since Mom left—"

"Keep her out of this." His jaw tightened as he gripped the curved edge of the sink.

She smoothed the frustration out of her voice and lowered her tone. "I'm only saying I'm here for you."

He sighed, then cracked a smile, looking more like the jovial Joe Bradley his customers saw on a regular basis. "Great, then grab a knife and give me a hand breaking down these vegetables. I need to make coleslaw for the Dinner with a Hero fund-raiser."

"What's that?" After washing and drying her hands, she pulled on a pair of disposable gloves, then snatched a sharpened chef's knife from the metal strip above the prep area, grabbed a few fat heads of cabbage out of the prep sink and lined them on the large cutting board at the prep station. After removing the outer leaves, she cut each of the heads in half and removed the cores, then shredded the cabbage quickly. She grabbed a bench scraper and scooped the large pile of cabbage into a stainless prep pan.

Dad scrubbed the carrots then julienned them with the skill and dexterity of a man who knew his way around a knife. "Tucker's late wife started it several years ago—community service men and women like police officers, firefighters, EMTs, etc., put together dinner baskets, then people bid on their baskets to eat dinner with a hero. The proceeds from the fund-raiser go toward helping families in need in the community."

"Sounds like a worthy cause. And people hire you to create their baskets?"

He chuckled. "Nah, they have to create their own baskets. I've been catering the event for the past couple of years—making food to serve for those who don't bid or lost their bids. Takes place on the Holland Farm. Besides the auction, there are information booths, vendors, games for kids, the works. It's become a community affair. You should go. Bid on a basket. Maybe you'll find your own hero."

"You're the only hero I need. Falling in love just leads to heartbreak. So, what are you making?"

"Keeping it simple this year with pulled pork, roasted chicken, potato salad, baked beans, coleslaw and chocolate chip cookies."

"Who's helping you?"

He shot her another grin. "Apparently you are now."

Isabella tightened her grip on the knife. "Dad, you're

doing too much. No wonder you passed out yesterday. You can't keep shouldering these burdens by yourself."

Dad waved his hands. "Look around, Bells. There's no one else. It's all on me."

"What happened to Sebastian? Or George? Or Larry?"

"Larry's in rehab after getting arrested for his second DUI. Sebastian has a family to support and couldn't afford to stick around a sinking ship after I had to cut his hours, so he bailed and found something more stable. George…well, he and I don't always see eye to eye, so no. I'd rather do it myself."

"You're his boss. If you're not happy with his performance, you need to let him go and hire someone else. But like I said—you're not doing things by yourself anymore. I'm here now and can help interview more responsible workers."

"Baby girl, you have a good heart, and I appreciate it, but like *I've* said—this is my problem. You focus on that fancy-pants restaurant of yours and I'll tend to this greasy spoon." He folded his arms over his chest and looked at her over the rims of his glasses. "Hey, by the way—what are you doing home midweek, anyway?"

Heat clawed at Isabella's neck and cheeks. She reached for another washed head of cabbage and broke it down quickly, scraping the chopped vegetables into another pan.

"Isabella…" He tipped up her chin and looked at her with knitted brows.

She tried to look away, but his gentle but firm touch kept her focused on him. Tears filled her eyes, and leaked down her cheeks.

Dad pulled her to his chest, wrapping her in a bear-size, comforting hug that always offered security.

Unable to hold back any longer, her shoulders shook

as her sobs soaked the front of his black Joe's All-Star Diner T-shirt. He kept her folded into his embrace and pressed a cheek against the top of her head. Then he pulled back and thumbed away her tears. "Tell me who I have to hurt."

She smiled, then told him about the wedding disaster that led to her humiliating firing and her conversation with Jeanne about the true cause of the bridesmaid's allergic reaction.

Dad handed her a clean towel, and she dried her cheeks, then covered her face a moment before taking a deep breath and looking at him. "So, you see—this was a blessing in disguise. If I hadn't gotten fired, then I wouldn't have come home and found you."

"And I'm grateful. I'm just sorry this happened to you. But don't let this Justin jerk tear you down. You're a great chef, Bells, and you deserve to work in a kitchen that appreciates your talents."

Isabella scoffed and resisted rolling her eyes. "Yeah, well, getting fired from a kitchen like the Briarwood tends to tarnish one's résumé, especially over a contamination issue. The frustrating part is, I know that pastry kitchen was safe. I made sure of it, but because one of the bridesmaids had a life-threatening reaction, somebody's head had to roll."

"I'm sorry she ended up in the hospital—I remember the first time you reacted to eating shrimp when you were five—but once they learned it wasn't your fault, Justin should've offered your job back."

"He had to save face. But I don't want to think about that right now. Let's talk about how we're going to turn the diner around."

She moved to the swinging door separating the kitchen from the dining area and took in the faded, worn booths, flat beige walls and wood paneling. She turned back to her father. "Hey, Dad, what if we updated? I mean, the food is great and all, but the decor hasn't changed since you bought the place when I was five. Maybe even add some new dishes to the menu. You'll be closed next week for your annual fishing trip, so I could spruce things up a bit."

He shook his head. "I can barely make payroll as it is. There's no extra money for updates. And with this loan past d—"

As if realizing what he'd just spilled, Dad clamped his jaw shut and turned back to the prep station.

She frowned. "What loan?"

"Nothing. Forget it."

"Let me help...as your business partner."

Raising an eyebrow, Dad gave her a pointed look. "My diner, my problem."

His constant use of "my" grated on her nerves. And stung just a little. When would he see her as more than his daughter—as someone who wanted to work alongside him?

"You're a prideful, stubborn man who is going to lose this place because you're not willing to accept help. What happened to this being our diner?"

"You're destined for greater kitchens than this greasy spoon." The resigned tone in his voice deflated her frustration.

Isabella drew in a breath and schooled her tone. She rested a hand on his arm. "Dad, I learned to cook by your side. You worked hard to put me through culinary school, so I'm blessed not to have student loans like many of my friends. I have money saved, so let me help."

"No!" Dad slammed his hand on the flat surface of the

prep sink, causing her to jump. "For the last time, this is my problem, and I will take care of it. Do you hear me?"

Tears filled her eyes again, but she blinked them back and steeled her spine. "No. We are a team. From the time Mom walked out, it's been you and me against the world. I could always count on you to have my back. If I hadn't come home last night, I could have lost you. So don't you tell me this is your problem." She wagged a finger between them. "This is our problem, and I'm going to help you save *our* diner whether you like it or not."

"And how do you plan to do that?"

"Let me update the place. Use social media to do some advertising. Expand our reach."

"It's a lot of change."

"If we don't change, we're not going to survive."

Dad looked at her a moment, then scrubbed his hands over his face, appearing a decade or two older than his fifty-five years. "Maybe you're right—maybe I should take it easy. I'm getting a headache. I'm going upstairs to stretch out for a bit."

"Dad…"

Without looking at her, he shuffled past, shoulders burdened and head down. The stairs outside the kitchen door creaked as he took them one at a time. A moment later, his footsteps sounded overhead, then stopped as she imagined him stretching out in his worn recliner in front of his TV.

Leaning against the prep sink, Isabella buried her face in her hands. Dad couldn't lose the diner. He just couldn't. He'd age faster than his years of overworking and shouldering responsibilities by himself. She could use her savings to invest in the diner, update the interior and do whatever else she could to help turn business around.

And put something toward his past-due balance…at least to bring the note current.

But would it be enough?

Problem was, she couldn't do it on her own, and after being away from home for so long, she didn't know whom she could call on to help.

She'd figure it out this weekend, put a plan in place, then be ready to reopen when her dad returned from his trip. Then she'd prove her value, and he wouldn't have any choice but to bring her in as his partner.

Tucker didn't feel like a hero.

Saving lives was just what he did.

At least for now.

But when the charity his late wife had started needed to raise money, he had to step up. No matter how he felt about the unwanted attention he received.

Now every year on the anniversary of his late wife's death, the Holland Family Farm was transformed into a community event that welcomed visitors from the tristate area. And no one seemed to mind the scents wafting off the pastures.

A warm October breeze carrying the scents of the farm stirred dried, crunchy leaves across the empty fields. The hillside patched with scarlet, gold and orange tagged the blue sky.

Due to his future sister-in-law's vision over the summer, one of their empty barns had been scoured from top to bottom, repaired and restored to be used for social events. According to Tori, barns were big venue items.

Vendors selling baked goods, craft items and T-shirts and community resource programs lined both sides of the barn.

A long line formed in front of Joe Bradley's food tent.

The scent of roasting chickens and smoked pork lingered in the air. Children's laughter and squeals could be heard from the small animal-petting area Dad and Claudia had set up.

Someone clamped a hand on his shoulder, and Tucker turned to find his older brother, Jake, standing behind him, wearing a navy Holland Family Farms Fatigues to Farming T-shirt from last month's fund-raiser for their new program to help veterans with disabilities find hope. Holding one of Joe Bradley's pulled pork sandwiches, the sweet and tangy scent of the barbecued meat permeating the wax paper, Jake nodded. "Hey, man. How's it going?"

Tucker lifted a shoulder. "They're raising plenty of money."

"When's it your turn?"

"Soon. They just finished auctioning off the city police department's baskets. The ambulance service is up next. I know this was Rayne's baby, but man, I hate being on display."

"But today's not about you. Sometimes you just gotta suck it up even when you don't like it."

"Oh, I know."

"Yeah, brother, you do. At least you have a good day to stand like a cow at auction." Jake elbowed him in the ribs.

"Thanks, dude, that makes all of this so much better."

"Just messin' with you, bro. You never know—you may end up winning over the girl of your dreams with your basket."

He shot his brother a look. "I had my happily-ever-after already, remember?"

"Dude, where did you get that lame idea? Tori and I reunited. Dad and Claudia found love again. You can, too."

"No one can compare to Rayne."

"She was one of a kind, but that doesn't mean you're

sentenced to spend the rest of your life alone. Only God knows what your future holds." Jake took a bite of his sandwich, then offered it to Tucker, who shook his head. "I have to get back inside the barn to our fund-raising booth, so Tori can bring Livie and Landon over when it's your turn. I just wanted to check in and see how you're doing."

"I'm fine."

Fine was subjective.

At least he had a plan B in place so he wouldn't be humiliated once the auctioneer started the bidding. He'd slipped Tori, Jake's fiancée, some money and asked her to bid on Landon's and Livie's behalf. That way, he could enjoy his kids' company without having to make awkward small talk.

Even though his late wife had started the Dinner with a Hero basket auction as a joke, no one had been laughing when they counted the generous proceeds afterward. Then the event became an annual thing to raise money for needy families in the community.

And Tucker never expected to be a recipient of the program.

So, of course, he needed to be there dressed in a pressed uniform with a smile pasted in place.

Captain Franco, his operations supervisor, turned and nodded to him, his cue to head onstage. "Next up, we have Tucker Holland, paramedic with the Shelby Lake ambulance service, widower and single father to Olivia and Landon. He owns Holland Family Farms with his father and three brothers. He's received numerous commendations for his quick thinking and lifesaving skills, and if that's not enough to whet your appetite, he's one of our very own hometown heroes, serving in the National

Guard for the past twelve years. Who will start the bidding at twenty-five dollars?"

Numbered auction paddles flew in the air, causing the auctioneer to increase dollar amounts at a rapid rate.

Tucker couldn't believe it.

"Do I hear one twenty-five? One hundred and twenty going once...going twice—"

"Two hundred dollars." A familiar female voice sounded from the back.

Gasps punctuated the air as Tucker scanned the crowd for the winning bidder.

Bella Bradley leaned against the corner of the barn with her paddle still in the air.

"Sold to the lovely Isabella Bradley for two hundred dollars. Enjoy your dinner, you two." Franco pounded a gavel against his portable podium.

Tucker reached for his picnic basket and made his way off the platform amid whistles and catcalls. The tips of his ears burned.

As he walked across the freshly cut field, he forced his steps to slow to a leisurely pace despite the desire to sprint across the grass. His stomach turned over as Bella lowered her paddle and raised her sunglasses to the top of her head to watch him with those honey-gold eyes.

Taking advantage of the unseasonably warm mid-October afternoon, Bella had dressed in a short-sleeved red Joe's All-Star Diner T-shirt, fitted jeans and tan ankle boots. Sunshine haloed her hair, stripping the dark brown to a light caramel.

She gave him a three-fingered wave as he approached.

He swept into a low bow and rolled his hand toward her. "Ma'am, your dinner companion awaits."

She laughed, a sound that zinged through him as she

jerked on his elbow. "Come on. Let's see what gourmet fare my hero is offering for two hundred bucks."

Tucker straightened and lifted the basket. "I promise you will not be disappointed."

Her gaze swept over the basket, then caught his eyes and lifted her chin. "Oh, I have no doubt."

He raised an eyebrow and bit down on a grin as her cheeks darkened. "Two hundred bucks? Seriously?"

"It's worth every penny, especially after what you did to save my dad's life. This is my way of saying thank you. Where do you want to go?"

"You choose. After all, it's your dinner."

Shielding her eyes, she pointed to sturdy oak losing most of its leaves. "How about under that oak? We'll have a little more privacy."

They crossed the field, leaving behind the noise of the crowds, blaring music from a local band playing a mix of music, and the auctioneer's rattle.

Tucker opened the picnic basket he'd borrowed from Claudia, pulled out a lightweight blue-and-green-plaid blanket, and spread it under the weighty branches.

Bella sat and braced herself on her arm as she peered into the open basket. She drew in a deep breath and exhaled, smiling. "Something smells great."

"Pork from the farm. Dad smoked it and then I shredded it and added spices and lime juice for carnitas tacos. We have corn or flour tortillas, lettuce, tomatoes, onions, cheese, avocado, and homemade salsa. And for dessert, some of Claudia's prize-winning apple crisp made with apples from our orchards. Not quite Mexican, but it's still great."

She rubbed her hands together. "My personal taco bar. Looks like I chose the right hero."

Tucker shook his head as he laid out the food. "I'm just an ordinary guy doing what needs to be done."

"Humble, too."

Desperate to change the subject and to douse his flaming ears, Tucker handed her a plate and waved for her to dig in.

"Everything looks so good." Bella spooned meat onto a hard corn shell and added toppings. She took her first bite, and sauce dripped through her fingers. "My former landlady was a widow from Mexico—Maria Flores Sanchez. She taught me how to make authentic Mexican cuisine, then Jeanne, my roommate, and I would attend church, then spend the afternoon hanging out with Maria's family."

"Speaking of family, how's your dad doing?" Tucker glanced over to the activity near the basket auction. "He's been pretty busy today."

The playful light in Bella's eyes dimmed as she set her half-eaten taco on her plate. "He's overdoing it as usual."

Tucker sipped from his water bottle. "What's going on?"

"The diner's in trouble—Dad accidentally let it slip about some loan being past due. He's going on his annual fishing trip next week, and since the diner's going to be closed, I'm going to repaint and update the dining room."

"How'd Joe take that?"

"He said he didn't have the money, and he had a fit when I offered to use my savings."

"So, what are you going to do?"

"I'm going to do it and prove to him I'm worth being his partner by helping to turn the business around."

"By yourself?"

"Yes. I don't have any other options. Dad's servers are

taking vacation at the same time. I've been gone for so long that you're the only one I know."

"Man, Bella, I wish I could give you a hand, especially since I owe your dad—"

She cut him off with a wave of her hand. "Dude, I wasn't asking, okay? And you don't owe my dad anything."

"He paid for my paramedic training and wouldn't let me pay him back."

"My dad likes you."

"And I like him. Which is why I'd love to help. Right now, though, I have to find a new nanny."

"What happened?"

Tucker explained about Mandy's broken engagement and abrupt resignation. "Landon and Livie's Aunt Willow is moving back to Shelby Lake in a few weeks, so I just need to find someone for the short term. Dad and Claudia are my last resort. She's finally convinced my dad to leave the farm and do some traveling, and I don't want them to feel obligated to shelve their plans to care for my kids."

"When do you work?"

"Sunday evenings at seven until Tuesdays around noon. That gives me the forty hours I need and allows me to spend as much time as possible with the kids."

"Sounds exhausting."

"When we're not out on a call, I can grab a nap at the station, catch up on paperwork or do homework." Tucker scraped a hand across his chin as an idea dawned on him. "How are you with children?"

Bella uncapped her water bottle and eyed him. "Why?"

"Well, you need help updating the diner in a week, and I need a temporary nanny for a couple of weeks. Maybe we can help each other out."

She dropped her gaze to her plate as she swirled a broken piece of her taco shell through his homemade salsa. "Oh, Tucker, I don't know. I mean, I love kids and you can trust me, but I have very little experience with them. I didn't even babysit in high school. You don't know what you're asking."

"I won't pressure you, but I do know I can trust you."

"What would you want me to do?"

"Basically, entertain them for a bit and help them get ready for bed. Then, in the morning, feed them and send them off to school."

"Seems easy enough."

Tucker smothered a laugh. No sense in discouraging her from the beginning. "Is that a yes?"

She released a sigh and nodded. "Sure, Tuck. I'll help you out."

He closed his eyes a moment as relief flooded through him. He fought back the urge to pull her into a hug. "Bella, you just made me the happiest man on the planet. I really appreciate it, and I'll help you whip the diner into shape. How about coming tomorrow after church to meet them? If you don't feel comfortable starting right away, then I'll ask Dad to keep them."

"I'll bring lunch, and we can talk more about what you want me to do, then I'll share my plans for the diner."

"Sounds good."

For the first time in several days, Tucker started to relax. Maybe, just maybe, things would work out after all.

Chapter Three

His family was going to think he'd lost his mind, but Tucker knew without a doubt he could trust Bella, even if he hadn't seen much of her in the past decade.

Joe had kept him posted on her accomplishments, and the pride in the older man's face had told Tucker all he needed to know. And after spending the afternoon with her, he was sure of his decision.

As he climbed the steps to the farmhouse to pick up Livie and Landon, the sweet scent of cooking apples mixed with cinnamon drifted through the open windows on either side of the front door.

Tucker reached for the handle, then hesitated. Until a couple of months ago, he'd come and gone as he pleased. The farmhouse had been the only home he'd known until he married Rayne soon after graduation and they'd settled in the ranch-style brick house down the road.

Then, after her death, he and the kids had moved back to the farmhouse temporarily.

For over two years.

Since Dad married Claudia nearly three months ago, though, Tucker hadn't felt comfortable just walking in unannounced, raiding the fridge or even leaving the kids at a moment's notice if he got called into work. No matter how much he loved Claudia, whom he'd always considered his second mom anyway, things were different now. And the newlyweds deserved their privacy.

But she'd also have his head if he rang the doorbell or knocked.

Country music blaring from the kitchen mingled with laughter as he stepped inside.

Claudia's laughter.

The woman had brought joy back to the farmhouse after years of grief from the tornado that had nearly destroyed their dairy farm and killed his mother. And for that, he'd always be grateful.

He palmed the kitchen doorjamb.

Two large stainless-steel stockpots full of apples bubbled and steamed on the five-burner stove. Dozens of sanitized jars sat on the kitchen table glistening in the late-afternoon sunshine streaming through the open window and casting rainbows across the cherry finish.

"Applesauce making. I knew I'd come at the right time. I'm surprised you have the energy after today's activities."

"Just in time to give us a hand filling those jars." Dad nodded toward the table as he picked up the metal potato masher and pressed it through the softened fruit.

"Hey, Tuck." Claudia paused coring apples long enough to stand on tiptoe to kiss his cheek. "I heard you had the largest bid at the auction today."

"Isabella Bradley saved me from an afternoon of small talk." He reached for an apple and tossed it from hand to hand. "Got a moment? I just wanted to let you know something."

Dad shot a quick glance at Claudia, and Tucker didn't

miss the look of concern that shadowed his eyes before he turned back to the stove.

Yeah, their family had gotten too good at sharing bad news over the past few years.

Dad turned down the heat under the pot, then leaned against the counter and crossed his arms over his chest. "Sure, what's up?"

Suddenly feeling drained after the busy day, Tucker dragged a hand through his hair. "Well, the thing is—"

The back door to the kitchen opened, cutting off Tucker's words. Jake and Tori entered with another basket of apples. Over their shoulder, Tucker saw Olivia and Landon holding flashlights they'd won at one of the games today and playing tag on the back deck with Meno on their heels.

"Hey, man." Jake dumped the apples in the sink, then looked at Claudia. "That's the last batch for this evening. It's getting too dark to pick."

"Hey, Tuck." Tori stood beside her fiancé and started washing the apples.

"Hi, guys. Thanks for keeping the kids today. Stellar job on partnering with the Dinner with a Hero event, City."

Tori grinned at his nickname for her due to lack of rural upbringing. "Thanks, Country Mouse." She returned her focus on the sink.

Jake grabbed a towel and dried his hands, shifting his eyes between his brother and his parents. "Did we interrupt something?"

Tucker picked up a long-handled metal spoon and stirred the bubbling sauce. "No, I was about to share some news with Dad and Claudia, and now that you two are here, it saves me from repeating it."

Jake leaned against the sink with his arms folded over his chest. "What's up?"

Tucker returned the spoon to the plate on the counter, pulled in a deep breath then exhaled slowly to gather his scattered thoughts. "Mandy quit, and Isabella Bradley's going to be caring for Olivia and Landon until Willow moves back home."

Claudia frowned, then picked up an apple and her paring knife. "You know that's not necessary. We can keep them until you can find someone more permanent."

"I appreciate that, C. I do. But you and Dad need your time together. And aren't you heading to Nashville this week for a few days? And Tori's returning to Pittsburgh for work this weekend."

"We can postpone. Family helps out one another. That's just what we do." Dad's voice, quiet and controlled, jerked Tucker's attention away from his stepmom.

"And lose out on the money for flights and hotel? No way."

Jake pushed away from the sink. "I thought Isabella was a chef at a high-end resort or something. What's she doing back in Shelby Lake? And didn't you two date in high school?"

"No, we were just good friends who worked together at Joe's. I'm not sure about her current job situation, but she and I talked earlier today. She's going to care for the kids until Willow returns, and I'm going to help her revamp her father's diner. Joe's been having a tough time lately, and she's home to lend him a hand."

Dad ran an open hand over his chin, then raised an eyebrow. "And when are you going to find time for that?"

"I'll make the time. Besides, it's only for a week."

Dad placed a hand on Tucker's shoulder. "I respect

your noble heart, son, but you can't rescue everyone just because they need help."

"This is different. After the tornado, Joe organized cleanup crews and fed us, remember? And saved my life. It's the least I can do."

Claudia curled her hand around his elbow. "I admire what you're doing, but are you sure this is the best solution?"

"This is only for a couple of weeks. I'm not asking her to marry me or anything. I've known Bella nearly my whole life."

He'd expected his family to go in protective mode, which they'd done since he moved back to his house and hired someone outside the family to care for his kids, but, man, could they at least trust he had some common sense? He made split-second lifesaving decisions on a daily basis, so why couldn't they see he'd thought this through?

Dad moved to the stove, gave the applesauce a final stir, then flicked off the heat. "Okay, then. What about the twins? Have you told them yet?"

Tucker shook his head. "Bella's coming for lunch tomorrow after church so they can all get to know each other. Honestly, Dad, I don't expect any problems."

Claudia set the fruit bowl on the counter, laid out a towel, then carried the jars one by one closer to the stove, where Dad seated a green canning funnel in place and ladled hot applesauce into them.

They worked together seamlessly without a word but in continual sync with each other's movements. That's what marriage was all about. And for a moment, Tucker's heart panged. He wanted that kind of in-sync partnership again. That unspoken ability to sense what the other needed without being voiced.

Claudia placed lids on the hot jars and screwed on the rings. Then she took a damp cloth and wiped away applesauce dripping down the sides. "Tucker, you have a good head on your shoulders, and you know what you're doing. Just remember—we're here to help in any way we can. Like your dad said—that's what family's all about, right?"

"Holland strong." Tucker made a fist and raised it, then glanced at the inside of his left forearm, where a tattoo of a heavy tree with tangled roots inked his tanned skin to symbolize that their family was strong and deep rooted enough to weather any storm together. He and his brothers had gotten matching tats after their mother's death.

Dad rested his hands on Claudia's shoulders. "We may bend, but we don't break."

He'd heard their family mantra all his life, and for so many years, he'd believed it. But man, the past few had tested his strength nearly to the breaking point. The weight of grief pressed on him so heavily at times that had it not been for his family's support, he wasn't so sure he would have been able to function.

But now he was holding on to hope for the next few weeks to go well, so when Willow moved back home to give him a hand, he could figure out what he needed to do to streamline his life so his supervisor would relax a bit.

Agreeing to trade services with Tucker was a mistake. What did Isabella know about caring for children?

What if Tucker's kids didn't like her? Then he'd be back to square one with his childcare problem, and she'd be without a helper and would have to handle the diner updates on her own. Scary thought.

She wielded a chef's knife better than a paintbrush. She had the paint-dipped-ponytail pictures to prove it.

Plus, she'd be letting Tucker down, and he didn't deserve that. The poor guy had it tough enough as it was. *Enough with the self-doubt already.*

Like everything else, she'd make this work, too.

Isabella pulled in the gravel driveway and took in the ranch-style brick home with the wide covered front porch, attached garage and hedges lining the front of the house. A basket of red geraniums swung from a wrought iron shepherd's hook next to the steps.

Two small bikes—one purple with tassels and one red with black racing stripes—lay on their sides in the grass next to a soccer ball and a single pink-and-white polka-dotted boot.

She stepped out of her car, retrieved a foil-covered baking dish and her purse, then forced her nerves to settle as she headed for the front door and rang the doorbell.

Barking and the pounding of feet sounded from inside the house. The red front door flew open, and she looked down into a miniature Tucker as a fluffy golden dog barked by his side.

She didn't need a photo album to remind her what Tucker had looked like as a child. The little boy sported the same dark blond hair that curled at the ends, blue eyes and impish grin as his father.

The dog stepped onto the porch and sniffed her. Seemingly satisfied, the animal turned and headed back into the house.

She returned her gaze at the child and smiled. "You must be Landon."

He nodded and cocked his head. "How do you know my name?"

"I know your dad, and he talks about you."

"Who are you?"

"I'm Isabella. I'm here to talk to your dad."

Still holding on to the doorknob, he turned and yelled, "Dad!"

Isabella bit back a smile. A moment later, a bleary-eyed Tucker appeared at the door, a crease in his cheek as if he'd fallen asleep. He stifled a yawn, then scrubbed a hand over his face. "Hey, Bella. Come on in."

She looked at him, then glanced at her car in the driveway. "Is this a bad time? I could come back."

He waved her inside, closing the door behind her. "No, it's fine. I was trying to do some studying, and I must've dozed off."

"Sounds like riveting material." She stepped inside, and the dog barked once again, wagging its tail.

"Meno, it's okay. Bella's harmless."

"Meno?"

"Livie and Landon named him after the clownfish in *Finding Nemo*, but they kept switching the consonants, and Meno stuck. Anyway, he belongs to my sister-in-law, Willow. We're dog-sitting while she's away."

"Beautiful dog."

"He's a goldendoodle—a cross between a golden retriever and a poodle."

Isabella held her hand out for Meno to inspect, then thrust the casserole dish at Tucker. "I made this for you."

He peeled back a corner of the foil and inhaled. "Smells fantastic. The twins ate right after church, so maybe we could save it for a bit."

His words loosened the cinched knot in her stomach. "Whenever. It even freezes well if you don't want it today. It's nothing fancy—baked herbed chicken tenderloin with rotini and vegetables in a creamy sauce. I tried to keep it simple and figured the kids would like the twirly pasta and cheese."

"As long as it doesn't contain mushrooms, we're

good." He carried the pan through the open dining room and into the kitchen, setting it on the stove.

She followed. "You don't like them?"

"I love them, but Landon's terribly allergic to them. And after what happened to Rayne, I don't even bring them into the house."

Isabella wanted to ask more, but she didn't want to make him uncomfortable. Or sad.

He snitched a noodle from the corner of the dish and popped it in his mouth. Closing his eyes, he groaned. "It's perfect. I want to dig in."

"Go for it."

"I'll give you a tour, then maybe you will join us?"

The earnestness in his eyes had her nodding before her brain could fire off a warning. Tucker was the one person who could get her to say yes to anything, which was why she was going to be caring for his children. Thankfully, he was a pretty upstanding guy.

"Great. Well, obviously, this is the kitchen." He waved a hand over the cream-colored cabinets, stainless appliances and gray-marbled countertops. He moved to a louvered door and opened it. "This is the laundry room and back door to the garage. We usually use this door when we're coming in or heading out. It's a two-stall garage, so feel free to park in there and come in through here."

They left the kitchen, headed down a short hall and stood in the doorway of a large room flooded with light from the bay window overlooking the backyard, which held a colorful swing set and hard plastic climb 'n slide. The dove-gray walls with white trim and a dark gray microfiber sectional sitting in front of a stone fireplace nestled between two built-in bookcases gave the room a homey feel. Textbooks, papers and a closed laptop lay on a square coffee table in front of the sectional. A large

TV hung above the mantel lined with family photos of Tucker and Rayne and Tucker, Rayne, Olivia and Landon.

Behind the couch, a pink-and-mint-colored play kitchen, a plastic workbench, a child-size table with two chairs, and shelves holding colored bins of toys and books had been arranged for a play area. Meno jumped up on the couch, his tail thumping against the cushion.

Tucker motioned for her to follow him down another hall off the dining room. He jerked his thumb at one of the closed doors. "That's my room."

He nodded toward two open doors across the hall. "These are the twins' rooms, and the door at the end of the hall leads to the bathroom. There's a trundle bed in Livie's room, where our previous nannies slept. If that won't work for you, let me know."

"I'm sure it will be fine." Isabella peeked into Landon's blue-and-red room and Livie's purple-and-green room, then turned back to Tucker. "You go in this evening and work until Tuesday at noon, right?"

Tucker nodded. "Yes, usually. Sometimes I'll get asked to stay over to cover other shifts. When that happens, though, it's usually spur of the moment and Dad keeps the twins. Which is why I don't want to ask him to care for them until Willow gets back. So, you're really helping me out."

"Sounds like we're helping each other out." They headed back to the dining room. "So, what are your expectations of me?"

"Keep my kids safe." He grinned, but there was an element of truth in his words.

He pulled out a dining room chair and gestured for her to sit. He sat across from her and folded his hands on the table. "If you could arrive by six thirty, that would give us a couple of minutes for debrief, then I'll head to work. Despite their insistence, the twins will need baths. No screen time, but they are allowed to play for a bit and read stories. They need to be in bed by eight thirty, even though they'll try to weasel more time. Then you're free to do whatever. Meno curls up on Landon's bed. In the morning, they need to be dressed, fed and ready to walk out the door by seven fifteen. I walk them to the end of the driveway and wait until they get on the bus. On my workdays, sometimes I'm able to make it home to see them for a couple of minutes before they leave. Once they're off to school, make sure Meno has fresh water and dry food, then lock the door and you're free to go. Oh, that reminds me…"

He dug in his pocket, pulled out his keys and twisted one off the ring and handed it to her. "Here's a house key for the side door leading into the garage. You think this will work for you?"

Taking it, she looked at it, the weight of his trust pressing into her skin. Forcing away any lingering doubts, she folded her fingers around the key. "As long as you're not expecting Mary Poppins."

"Nah, I've heard your British accent." He winked, then reached for her hand. "I've known you my whole life, and like I told you yesterday—I trust you."

Holding on to his words, she smiled. "This schedule will give me time to get things done at the diner before Dad gets back. Hopefully, once we reopen, he'll be back to his old self again and we can move forward."

"Still discouraged?" Tucker headed into the kitchen and pulled four plates out of the dishwasher.

Isabella took them and set the table. "And grumpy and frustrated. I'm hoping his new medicine will help stabilize his blood sugar and improve the moodiness."

"Give it time. Diabetes isn't something to mess around

with, so I'm glad he has you looking out for him." Tucker left the kitchen and called the kids in from the backyard and directed them to the bathroom to wash their grubby hands.

They raced into the house, elbowing one another to be the first in line. Landon wore a bath-towel cape, and Olivia wore a glittery pink tutu over a unicorn hoodie.

As Olivia rushed past, Isabella plucked a leaf from her windblown blond hair.

"Ow!" Grabbing her head, the little girl whirled around, shooting an accusatory look at Isabella, then turned her attention to Tucker. "Daddy, she pulled my hair."

Isabella's cheeks heated as she looked at the dry leaf in her hand. "I'm sorry, honey. I didn't mean to. I was simply removing the leaf."

"My name is Olivia Lillian Holland." She snatched the leaf from Isabella and slapped it back on her hair. "And I wanted that leaf there."

Tucker dropped to his haunches and reached for his daughter's hand. "Well, Miss Olivia Lillian Holland, in this house, we show kindness to others. And you're being very rude. You owe Bella an apology."

"But I don't want to." Her bottom lip protruded as tears filled her eyes.

"I didn't ask if you wanted to. Bella didn't hurt you on purpose, but your words and sassy attitude are not okay. I'll wait until you're ready to apologize."

Landon nudged his sister. "Hurry up, Livie. I'm hungry."

Tucker shot his son a look. "Landon."

The boy rolled his eyes and trudged down the hall. Tucker returned his attention to Olivia, watching silently and waiting.

"Daddy…"

"Livie…"

Isabella edged a step closer to the door. "Maybe I should go."

Tucker reached for her hand, his rough skin warm against hers. "No."

"Livie, Bella is one of my very best friends. I've known her since I was your age. How would you feel if Bridget and Addie came over to play and I said grumpy things to them?"

Olivia's hands flew to her face. "Oh Daddy, I would be so 'barassed."

Tucker bit his lip and nodded. "Exactly. Now, what do you say to Bella?"

Olivia's cheeks reddened as her eyes darted between her father and Isabella, then she lowered her lashes. "Sorry for using my grumpy voice."

Isabella smiled and touched her cheek. "Thank you for saying that, and I forgive you. I use my grumpy voice sometimes, too. My name's Isabella, and I think we will become good friends."

"Are you going to be our new mommy?"

Isabella gave her a startled look. "What? No. Why do you ask that?"

"Because you and my daddy are holding hands the way Uncle Jake holds Tori's hand."

Isabella dropped Tucker's hand as if it were on fire and clasped hers behind her back.

Tucker laughed, a warm, rich sound that flowed through Isabella. "Bella will be caring for you while I'm working until Auntie Willow returns from her trip."

Olivia's bottom lip trembled. "I miss Mandy. And Auntie Willow."

Tucker wrapped her in his arms. "I know you do,

sweetheart. Let's eat, then we'll take Bella down to visit the farm."

Olivia's face brightened as she scrambled out of his embrace and headed for the bathroom. Tucker prayed over the food, then dished up the kids' plates.

Thirty minutes later, and after telling Isabella twice to leave the dishes, Tucker ushered the four of them out the door and into the afternoon sunshine. Isabella stuffed her hands in the front pocket of her pullover hoodie and wished she'd brought a jacket to wear over her long sweat-shirt and leggings.

The twins ran ahead, Landon's cape flowing behind him and Olivia's unicorn horn bobbing as she moved. Olivia stopped to pick some purple flowers growing alongside the road, then held them out to Isabella.

"Thank you. Purple's my favorite color."

"Mine, too." Olivia looked at her shyly, then fell in step with Isabella and Tucker instead of running ahead to catch up with her brother.

Maybe Isabella didn't need to be Mary Poppins or have a degree in early childhood education. After all, she could totally relate to the motherless young child on so many levels. And perhaps that was the key to build-ing this relationship.

Hope bloomed in her chest, filling her with excitement for the first time since agreeing to Tucker's suggestion. After all, it was only for a couple of weeks. She could handle it for Tucker's sake…and for her own.

Chapter Four

Isabella needed to up her game.

Otherwise she wasn't going to meet her deadline to have the diner ready for the grand reopening on Monday.

Still kneeling and holding the pry bar he'd used to remove the baseboard molding, Tucker sat back on his heels and wiped the back of his hand across his forehead. "Bella, either you're wearing some sort of superhero costume under that pink T-shirt and your jeans, or you've seriously overestimated my abilities. We're going to need more than a week to get everything done."

With his faded blue baseball hat on backward, faded Levi's and red V-neck T-shirt that showed every muscle in his back when he moved, Isabella struggled to keep her attention on the wall she'd been painting.

Standing on a ladder with a paintbrush in her hand, Isabella looked down at him. "Well, that's all the time we have. Everything needs to be done by Sunday evening."

"Does your dad know what you have planned?"

"Not specifically, but he bought the paint and flooring a while ago and told me to use it instead of wasting money on something new."

"He's pretty set in his ways. So are his customers."

"And look where that's got him. He hasn't raised his prices in years, and now, thanks to some mystery debt he won't talk about, he's about to lose everything. Set or not, something needs to change. It might as well be the wall color." Her voice cracked on the last words as she climbed down the ladder.

Perfect. Now she was crying in front of him.

A wave of fatigue washed over her, pressing down on her shoulders.

Caring for the twins took way more energy than she had expected. Once she'd gotten them into bed, she'd stayed up way too late making plans for the diner, and then she couldn't sleep on Livie's trundle bed. Thankfully, she could sleep in her own bed tonight, but she didn't expect to rest until the diner was ready for reopening on Monday.

In the meantime, she needed to find the energy to finish the walls she'd been painting since eight o'clock yesterday morning.

Tucker took two steps to her, then pulled her against his chest. "Hey, I'm sorry. I'm not trying to be a downer or anything. I just hate to see you pushing yourself like this."

Her arms slid around his waist as he tightened his hold. She breathed in the scent of his fabric softener. "I'll be fine. Dad's the one I'm worried about. He's still so tired and run-down. I'm not so sure he should've gone on that fishing trip, but he hasn't missed it in ten years. Maybe the time on the water will do him some good. So, I'll do what I can to help while he's gone."

She moved away from Tucker reluctantly and slid the ladder over to the next section of ceiling trim that needed to painted. "Dad does no advertising, and when I asked him about social media, he muttered about not knowing anything about 'Facechat or Tweeter.' The man still uses a flip phone. I'm working with a friend to create a web-site. I'm setting up social media accounts and designing new menus with some healthier food options."

Tucker eyed her. "Please tell me you're keeping Joe's famous garbage fries."

She wrinkled her nose. "Ugh, those artery-clogging things *should* be in the garbage. I'm not changing most of Dad's food, but I am simplifying the menu, cutting out higher-costing products that aren't ordered often enough and adding lighter, healthier options. Not everything needs to be swimming in grease. But do you mind if we keep talking while we work? I want to get the rest of this trim painted."

Tucker snapped his legs together, slammed his arms to his sides, then gave her a tight salute. "Ma'am, yes, ma'am."

"At ease, Sergeant Sarcasm."

"That's Staff Sergeant Sarcasm, ma'am."

"That's great! When did you pick up your stripe?"

"During my two weeks of training over the summer—after the Fatigues to Farming fund-raiser that Tori organized. That's how she and Jake got back together."

"How do you juggle everything with your family, your job, school, helping on the farm and the National Guard?"

Tucker lifted a shoulder. "Rayne and I wanted to get married after graduation, but Dad required us to have some sort of military service, and the National Guard Reserves allowed me to do that without being away from my family. Plus, I can retire in less than ten years now and draw a secondary income. It's not always easy, but it works for me."

"You're pretty amazing."

He shook his head. "I'm nobody special. Just trying

to keep my head above water while raising my kids the best I can."

"Well, you're a great dad, Tucker. Everything else will fall into place."

He cleared his throat. "Are we going to work or what?"

For the next fifteen minutes, the creak of separating wooden baseboards from the wall and the swishing of Isabella's brush as it glided over the narrow wood mingled with the mix of country and contemporary Christian music playing from Tucker's phone.

Every now and then he'd sing along with the music, and Isabella paused her painting to listen to his rich baritone.

Needing a break, Isabella climbed down the ladder and crossed to the breakfast counter, where her notebook lay. She leafed back to the beginning pages, where she'd drawn a map of the restaurant, then she tapped her foot against the chipped black-and-white-tiled floor. "Replacing this dated tile with that laminate wood flooring will a great improvement."

Tucker stood and rubbed his lower back. "Dated? Don't you mean retro?"

"If we were reproducing a '50s-style diner, then it would be perfect, but honestly, that doesn't feel like Dad's personality. He wasn't even alive in the '50s."

"Well, I like what you've done so far."

"By priming and painting over that hideous wood paneling with the barn red and using a milky white for the top half, I'm pulling in sort of an Americana feel, especially with the colonial blue for trim work. Since Dad loves the hometown feel of the diner, I want to hang framed and matted photos of different parts of the community—the lake, of course, downtown, the park, your family's farm if they'll let me—taken by local photog-

raphers." She turned and faced the front of house service station. "Dad loves to fish and be outside, especially
at the lake or in his garden, whenever he can. But with
running the restaurant, he doesn't get to do that often,
so I'd like to mount some of his old fishing gear around
the pass-through window along with framed photos from
his fishing trips."

Moving toward the empty back wall, Bella waved her
hands over the space. "I'd like to highlight our hometown
heroes—active-duty military, veterans and community
service workers—on this back wall. What do you think?"

Tucker seemed to be taking his time in answering,
which didn't help with the growing pit in Isabella's stomach. "I think your ideas are great…"

"I hear a 'but' coming."

"Seriously, I think it's great, but again, I'm just not
so sure how you're going to get everything done in less
than a week."

With a hand on her hip, she glanced at her check-
list. "I finished painting the walls yesterday, and I'll be
done with all of the trim work today. I'll have everything
moved out of the way so we can lay the flooring tomorrow. I paid for expedited shipping for the new booths to
arrive by Friday, so I can spend a day getting those in
place. Then it's a matter of hanging the pictures, which
will be ready by Saturday."

"Now I know you're definitely a superhero in disguise."

Isabella rolled her shoulders and reached for her bottle
of water. "Hardly. I make a plan and stick with it until the
job is done. This may not be the French bistro I'd love
to have someday with lots of light, cute tables, hanging
plants, a small bakery and daily specials, but this place
makes Dad happy, so for now I will be content. Like I

said, I want to show Dad I'm good enough to be a part of this place."

"Hey, now. I don't think your dad ever felt you weren't good enough. In his mind, it's quite the opposite—he feels you're destined for bigger and better things."

"Then why do I still feel less than?"

"Because those are lies in your head getting in the way of who you truly are."

"He won't let me help him." She toyed with the corner of her notebook, creasing the page and smoothing it out. Then she smiled and rested a hand on his arm. "Enough of my pity party. Anyway, thanks, Tuck. I really appreciate this. You have no idea what it means to me."

He lifted a shoulder. "Hey, I'm just a guy standing in front of a pretty girl and asking her to find the flooring."

Laughing, she slugged him playfully on the shoulder. "How about I show you where it is and let you be my muscle? I've never installed a floor before, but I've been watching some YouTube videos."

"I've installed plenty of flooring. Once I get the rest of these baseboards off, then we can clear everything out of the way and snap the boards in place."

"I know this is off-topic, but I wanted to talk to you about something."

"What's up?"

"Spending time on your family's farm yesterday sparked an idea. Of course, I need to do more research and talk to Dad, but I'd like to consider buying some local meats and produce for the restaurant. It will help boost the economy, support farms such as yours, and I believe our customers will like knowing some of their food products come from our local farming community. There are pros and cons we need to weigh before doing it, but I'm wondering if it's something we can move toward. You mentioned needing to come up with a project for part of your property to benefit the Fatigues to Farmers project, right?"

"Yes, that was one of the stipulations when Dad divided the property between my brothers and me. Why? What are you thinking?"

"What about a community garden? The veterans and their families could coordinate with Shelby Lake residents and sell the produce at the farmers market and local restaurants, with the proceeds benefitting the program. There will be some licensing requirements, but it could be another facet of the program that could build a bridge with the community."

"While I like the idea, I'm just not sure where I'll have the time to oversee it."

"How about asking my dad?"

"Joe? You think he'd be interested?"

Isabella shrugged. "He's a veteran who loves gardening and this community. Maybe it will give him another purpose…something to pull him out of this depression. If you talk to him, he may be more receptive."

He considered her words for a moment, then smiled. He brushed a finger along her jaw. "I don't know what good it will do, but I'll do it for you."

The way he smiled and the warmth in his words curled around Isabella's heart and nestled in place. If she wasn't careful, she could find herself falling in love with Tucker Holland. And that would be a disaster. She didn't know if she could handle losing her heart to him twice and still survive.

"What's going on in here?"

At the sound of her father's raised voice, Isabella whirled around and found her dad standing in the doorway between the kitchen and dining room dressed in

faded jeans, a worn red-and-blue flannel shirt, and his
olive drab fishing vest hanging unzipped.

"Dad, what are you doing here?"

"I live here."

"I know, but I thought you were fishing until Saturday."

"Wasn't feeling well, so I came home early."

Oh, Dad.

He took another step into the room and frowned.
"You've been busy."

"I wanted to surprise you."

"I'm surprised, all right."

The ragged edges of his voice created a knot in her
stomach. She'd wanted to surprise him with the make-
over, but now that he was back…well, she'd have to try
and finish without getting in his way.

Tucker wasn't sure what Bella had hoped he could ac-
complish by talking with her father, but being a man of
his word, Tucker had to give it his best shot.

The way Isabella looked at him with those vulnerable eyes, he would've agreed to doing almost anything.
Being around her was going to get him into trouble if he
wasn't careful.

And if Joe was willing, then this could be the solution
Tucker needed to get Jake off his back.

He loved his brother. He did. But, man, he needed
some room to just…breathe.

After Tucker had shared Isabella's idea about the community garden for the veterans enrolling in the Fatigues
to Farming program, Jake was all over him trying to
make it happen.

However, getting Joe to agree to oversee the project
was going to be a long shot at best.

When Tucker had checked on Joe at the hospital, his friend had chewed him out about letting Bella know about the problems with the diner, so he wasn't high on Joe's list of favorite people right now.

Tucker rounded the back of the diner to find Joe crouched in his small garden, the afternoon sun beating on his back. "Hey, Joe. What's going on?"

The older man looked up as he picked a plump red tomato off the vine. "Picking the last of the tomatoes before I put the garden to bed for the winter. You want to crush those, too?"

Tucker sighed and kicked a clump of dirt with the toe of his loafer. "No one's crushing anything. You should've been honest with your daughter from the beginning, then my slipup wouldn't have been an issue. As for repainting the diner, we're doing it to help you—to help the business."

"No one asked you to." He continued picking, his back to Tucker.

"Actually, your daughter did."

"She had no business doing that."

"You know, Joe, we can go back and forth about that all day and neither one of us will see the other's point, so let's agree to disagree. Besides, I came to talk to you about something else."

"About what?"

"See that plot of land that borders your property?" Tucker pointed over Joe's head at the acreage between his house and the diner.

Joe nodded. "What about it?"

"Well, as I'm sure you know, I own it. After the tornado nearly destroyed the farm and killed Mom, Dad divided the farm by five, giving each of us boys a piece of the property with the condition we use a portion of our properties for the Fatigues to Farming program. When Bella visited yesterday, she suggested a community garden. Dad, Jake and I talked it out, and we think it's a great idea. Problem is, with my schedule, I don't have time to coordinate it. With your love of gardening and experience with veterans, we wondered if you'd be willing to oversee the project."

"And you think I have time?" Joe stood, straightened, then winced as he pressed a hand against his lower back. "Working six days, I've got my hands full with the diner. There's no time for anything else."

"But you have Bella here now to help."

"That girl doesn't belong here. She's a classically trained chef, not a fry cook. She's just home long enough to let her wounds heal, then she'll be gone again."

The wistful tone in Joe's voice tore at Tucker's gut. But he was kind of beginning to feel the same way. Although he still didn't know what had brought Bella home, he wasn't ready for her to leave again.

And that admission shook him a little more than he wanted to admit. He didn't want to think of her as more than a friend. Otherwise, he was setting himself up for more heartache. And he'd had enough to last a lifetime.

"What do you know about community gardens, anyway?" With a half bushel basket wrapped in his beefy arm, Joe pushed his hat up and scratched the top of his head.

"Not much, but Bella seems to think you do. She mentioned you overseeing one years ago when you were married to her mom."

Joe waved away his words. "That was a long time ago. Things change. People change."

Tucker wasn't sure what to make of the older man's

cryptic comment. "The farm wants to break ground for a community garden for the veterans and their families to begin in the spring when the Fatigues to Farming program launches, and we thought maybe you'd be willing to meet with Dad, Jake and me to talk about setting it up and coordinating the project."

"Why not ask one of the veterans coming in to the program?"

"Because they're going to be too new. Besides, you can be their community connection. You know practically everyone."

Joe eyed him a moment, then shook his head. "Sorry, man. I can't do it. Not right now. You need to find someone else."

"At least think about it." Tucker glanced at his watch, then shoved his hands in his pockets.

"You don't give up, do you?"

"Not really—kind of comes in handy when trying to save lives."

"Well, you can forget about this conversation because you need a leader for that kind of project, and I'm not one."

Tucker flung a hand toward the diner. "Joe, you've run this diner single-handedly for twenty-five years. How can you not think you're a leader?"

"A leader wouldn't run his business into the ground."

"All you had to do was ask for help."

Joe shook his head. "My diner. My problem."

"Your stubborn pride. Bella's worried, you know."

"Whose fault is that? If you hadn't told her, she wouldn't have anything to worry about."

"And if she hadn't come home when she did, then you wouldn't be standing here arguing with me." Tucker schooled his tone and held out a hand. "Let me help, Joe. You've been like a second dad to me. After the tornado, you fed us for days and spearheaded the cleanup crew. Not to mention saving my life when I wrecked my car in front of the diner when I was seventeen. Without your quick thinking, I would've died. I owe you."

"Son, you owe me nothing. You have your hands full with those kiddos of yours."

"At least consider the community garden. Your chili wins the cook-off every year, and it's because of those homegrown tomatoes of yours."

"That's not enough reason for a community garden."

"How about because I'm asking? You have a better connection with the vets than I do. I never saw combat. And maybe we could use the produce from the garden in the diner."

"Being a reservist isn't any less than serving in Desert Storm. And we can't use produce in the diner that hasn't been inspected by the USDA. You should know that."

"You're right." Tucker sighed and shoved his hands in his front pockets. "Okay. I get it. I'll let you get back to your tomatoes."

Tires crunched on the gravel in the back parking lot. Bella exited her car and walked toward him, a smile lighting up her face. "Hey, guys. What's going on?"

His heart gave a little jump, which was totally unexpected. What was that about? He shrugged it off. "I tried talking your dad into overseeing the community garden, but he turned it down."

"Why, Dad?"

"Would you two just back off? I said no, okay? Let it go." Joe grabbed his basket and headed for the diner.

Bella watched him leave with sadness rimming her eyes, and once he disappeared inside, she turned to

Tucker. "I'm sorry. I really thought he'd go for it, but it seems I was wrong. Dad's been…different since I've been home."

"Different how?"

"I don't know. He's been more snappish, grumpy and harder to get along with. He's always been so easy-going—I don't know what to make of this change. I feel like he doesn't want me here."

"Diabetes can cause some changes in a person. Many people with it may experience depression, mood swings and other things. You may want to talk to his doctor and see about making sure his medication stays regulated."

"Yeah, like he'll give me that kind of information. Due to HIPAA laws I can't ask anything without Dad's permission, and he's so guarded that I doubt they'll let me. We'll get through it. We always do."

"But at what cost?"

"I'm stronger than I look. I can take it."

"I'm glad caring for two rambunctious five-year-olds hasn't scared you off."

"Even though I haven't spent a lot of time with kids, it's been good."

"Have I mentioned how much I appreciate you?" Tucker dropped an arm around her shoulders and gave her a light squeeze.

Before Bella had arrived to care for them, he'd talked with Livie and Landon to ensure they were on their best behavior. And so far, everything had been working out.

Almost too good to be true.

Almost.

He knew his children well, but Bella was right—she was much stronger than she looked. And for that, he was grateful.

But now he was the one who needed to be strong and remember Bella's time in Shelby Lake was temporary— and he couldn't afford to lose his heart.

Chapter Five

One more hour until bedtime.

She could do it.

Two five-year-olds wouldn't wreck her.

She was stronger than that.

Wasn't that what she'd told Tucker earlier that afternoon?

When Tucker called in a slight panic to say he'd gotten called into work to cover a shift and didn't have anyone else to help, Isabella had rinsed her paintbrushes and headed to his house. Then after learning the kids hadn't eaten dinner yet, Isabella had reminded him she could handle her way around the kitchen.

After all, most kids liked pasta, right?

Apparently not Olivia and Landon. At least not the homemade kind Isabella had whipped up. They wouldn't touch it because the cheese was white, not orange. Then attempts at making something else caused Olivia to dissolve into tears because Isabella hadn't made her PB&J correctly.

At least bath time made her smile again.

Isabella rinsed the soap crayon artwork off the bathtub wall, gathered the basket of colorful plastic food and dishes Livie insisted on needing in her bath, then drained the pink water.

Two baths completed in less than ninety minutes.

Now to get the little monkeys into bed.

After agreeing to help Tucker out, she'd binged on parenting blogs, hoping to gain some insight into caring for the kids. The parenting gurus talked about establishing bedtime routines for a peaceful transition.

All good in theory, but did those authors even have children? Or rambunctious ones like Olivia and Landon?

From somewhere down the hall, Olivia screamed, then raced into the bathroom wearing a purple nightgown with a ruffled hem. Meno barked and raced beside her.

Slamming the door, Olivia pressed her back against it as tears coursed down her cheeks. She pushed wet, tangled hair off her face as sobs shuddered her chest.

Landon pounded on the other side of the door, causing Meno to bark even louder. "Let me in, Livie."

"No, you're being mean. I don't like you."

Isabella smothered a sigh and dried her hands on one of the damp bath towels puddled on the floor. "What's going on with you two?"

"Landon's being a meanie."

"Am not!"

"Are too."

"Okay, enough." Wrapping an arm around the child's shoulders, Isabella moved her aside and opened the door. She took Liv's hand and reached for Landon's. "Both of you come with me."

She walked them to the living room, sat on one half of the gray microfiber sectional and patted cushions on each side of her. Meno jumped up on the couch, then climbed over Isabella to claim an empty spot at the other end. "Time for a little chat."

The twins climbed up and sat next to her. For half a second, Isabella claimed it as a victory. "New rule—"

Landon groaned. "Rules are no fun."

She tried not to let his words sting as she ruffled his still-damp hair. "Everyone needs rules, my man. Otherwise, we'd have nothing but chaos."

"What's chaos?"

Isabella glanced at the plastic farm animals, baby dolls, pink-and-purple tea set, building blocks, and toy cars scattered across the hardwood floor in front of the stone fireplace.

Chaos seemed to be her new adventure.

"Chaos happens when everyone does what they want, when they want, and ignores the rules. Rules keep us safe and protected. So, here's a new rule—you're allowed to get mad at each other, but saying you don't like one another is not okay. Got it?" She grabbed a tissue, cupped Olivia's chin and dried her eyes. "It's so important to love your brother all the time, even when he's being a meanie."

Olivia stuck out her bottom lip. "But he threw that icky snake on me again."

Isabella turned to Landon and gave him a firm look. "Dude. We talked about that snake twice already. And what did I say?"

He scrunched up his face and heaved a sigh. "If I did it again, you were going to take it away."

"That's right, so hand it over."

Landon flung himself back on the couch and moaned. "No fair."

"It wasn't fair to tease your sister."

"She's just being a baby."

"Am not." Livie stuck out her tongue.

Landon returned the gesture. "Are too."

Isabella held out her hand. "Landon."

Muttering under his breath, he dropped the realistic-looking rubber snake in the palm of her hand, and she swallowed a shriek. No sense in giving him more power. She stuffed it behind a blue-and-white-striped pillow and glanced at the clock. "Now it's time for a story, then bed."

"Bed? But it's too early. Daddy lets us stay up."

"You have school tomorrow." Isabella dropped a kiss on Livie's forehead. "You two have had a long day and need some sleep."

"I'm not tired." Landon rubbed his eyes with a fist.

"Then you can rest in your bed and think happy thoughts until you fall asleep. Now, grab a book and I'll read to you."

They scurried off the couch, raced to the small bookshelf and pulled off books until they found the ones they wanted and then ran back to Isabella, leaving the discarded books in a haphazard heap on the floor.

Isabella swallowed the lecture burning her tongue. Tomorrow would be here soon enough. They could talk about cleanup then. Bedtime was in sight. She could make it through two stories.

Then she'd finish cleaning up and spend an hour or so working on a new business plan for the diner. If she could stay awake that long.

Repainting and climbing up and down ladders used more muscles than she realized she'd had.

Once the twins settled on either side of her, Isabella read stories about cats and fish. Then she tucked them into their own beds, listened to their prayers that didn't seem to end, turned off lights, then returned to the living room, where she collapsed on the couch.

She'd sit for five minutes before cleaning up the mess in the bathroom and the toys in the living room, get the dishwasher running, and then she'd open her computer.

A touch on her arm, and she looked down. Landon's rubber snake, with its jaws open, stared at her. She screamed and threw the snake across the room. Meno barked and bounded off the couch to retrieve it.

For half a minute, Isabella considered burying it in the trash, but she couldn't do that to Landon. Instead, she tossed it under the couch and made a mental note to have Tucker take care of it.

With Meno stretched out beside her, Isabella rested her head against the pillow and reached for a pale yellow afghan. One the twins had informed her their mother had knitted it when she was pregnant with them.

A story Tucker must have told them.

No wonder he had moved back to the farmhouse after Rayne's death.

Every room whispered of her presence—from the shiplap wall in the kitchen to the framed photos of her and the twins scattered around the house. Even the very faint scent of lavender that escaped from the linen closet in the bathroom.

Isabella had always liked Rayne, but once she and Tucker had started dating, Isabella had kept her distance, because seeing them together all the time created an ache in her chest that never really went away.

Now, being in the house where they had raised a family together, some of those pangs of jealousy had resurfaced.

And the shadow of Rayne's presence seemed to follow Tucker, who was still in love with his late wife.

She couldn't compete with that. So, she'd stay strong for the remaining time she had to care for his children, and for the help he was offering at the diner.

Her heavy eyelids drooped. She'd rest for just five minutes, then get to work with cleaning up the messes.

Something soft brushed against Isabella's chin. She batted at it, coming in contact with a warm hand. Her eyes jerked open, and she found Tucker dressed in his uniform leaning over her with the afghan in his hand. She must have knocked it on the floor. She sat up quickly, then swayed slightly when her head started spinning.

"Whoa, take it easy." Tucker reached for her upper arms and guided her back against the pillow. "How's it going?"

His voice, rich and velvety, washed over her. She shifted into a sitting position and pushed her hair out of her face. "What's wrong? Why are you home so early? I thought you had a twenty-four-hour shift."

"Early? It's after midnight."

"Midnight? Oh man…" Isabella dragged a hand through her hair. "I didn't mean to fall asleep. The bathroom is a wreck. The dishwasher needs started. There are toys everywhere."

"Those things can wait. You need to get some sleep."

"Tomorrow will have even more work to do." Isabella pushed off the couch and picked up the afghan to fold it. "I'll get things picked up here, then get some sleep. You didn't answer me—what are you doing home?"

"I tried to check in to see how your evening had gone and to say good-night to the kids, but you didn't answer your phone or the texts I sent, so I got worried. We didn't have much going on, so I came home to check on you."

She picked up her phone and saw the notifications of missed texts and phone calls. His care and concern filled her with warmth. When had someone cared enough to check on her without wanting anything in return?

"I'm sorry I worried you. My phone was on silent." She opened her arms. "As you can see, I'm fine. We played a game after supper, then the kids had baths, two stories, then bed." Burdening Tucker with the snake issue could wait. "I planned to get this mess cleaned up then do some social media work for the restaurant for a bit, but we can see how well that turned out."

"Don't push yourself so hard, Bella. Things will come together in God's timing."

Isabella didn't want to hurt Tucker's feelings or mock his faith, but she believed in having a plan and working hard to make it happen. Instead, she shifted the conversation back to his children. "After I send them off to school, I'm going to head back to the diner, so let me know if you need anything."

"Thanks. I appreciate everything you're doing to help us out. And to think you were nervous about caring for them." He glanced at his watch. "I gotta go—I just wanted to check in really quick to make sure the house was still standing. See you in the morning."

Barely, but they'd made it through. Maybe this would work out after all. It had to. Tucker and her dad—whether he wanted to admit it or not—were counting on her. She couldn't afford to let either of them down.

Tucker didn't like the dark shadows bruising Bella's eyes, and he felt to blame.

But he'd been around women long enough to know commenting on their less-than-stellar appearance meant bad news for him. And he enjoyed staying out of the doghouse.

But, man, Bella looked like she was ready to drop even after sleeping all night. Well, that was, if she had slept after he stopped by to check on her.

And now as he stood in the doorway of the kitchen, an appreciation he couldn't even put into words rose up within him. In just a matter of days, she'd made a huge difference with his family. Livie and Landon talked about her constantly, asking for her to come back even when he wasn't working. He took that as a win.

Flour dusted the countertop near the stove, and bowls and spoons filled the sink. At the dining room table, Olivia and Landon chattered around bites of syrup-drenched speckled pancakes. Bella listened as she clutched a steaming cup of coffee.

"Hey, did you save any pancakes for me?"

Bella jumped, then gave him a weary smile. She wore gray yoga pants, a long-sleeved pink T-shirt and had her hair twisted in some sort of messy bun. And she couldn't have looked cuter.

Forks clattered against their plates as the twins scrambled off their chairs and hurled themselves at him, "Daddy! Guess what? Izzie let us make pancakes."

Izzie?

Olivia flung out her arms. "Real ones. Not the box kind."

"Or the frozen toaster ones."

Tucker laughed and wrapped an arm around each of them. "Bella is pretty talented, isn't she?"

She rose from the table, refilled her cup, then poured coffee into a John Deere mug and handed it to him.

"Bless you, woman." He released his kids and reached for the cup, taking a sip. "Oh man, I could get used to this."

She peered at him over the rim of her mug. "Someone to serve you coffee?"

He waved a hand at the messy kitchen and laughing children. "This. All of it. A great-smelling kitchen. Happy, smiling kids." He raised his eyebrow. "And yes, a beautiful woman serving me coffee."

She lowered her eyes, but pink stole across her cheeks.

She looked at him over the rim. "But this is only temporary, right?"

Her words echoed inside his head.

Yes, their agreement was only temporary, but the more he was around Bella, the more he wanted to make it permanent.

And that was just crazy. He couldn't fall in love with her.

Not when she'd been back in his life for such a short amount of time.

Bella set her mug on the counter and opened the fridge. She pulled out the kids' lunch boxes and set them on the table next to their now-empty plates. "You two need to rinse your plates, put them in the dishwasher, then get your teeth brushed. The bus will be here shortly."

"Okay, Izzie." Livie and Landon scooted off their chairs and carried their plastic Disney character plates and matching cups to the sink where Isabella stood and turned on the water.

To Tucker's amazement, they did as she'd said and placed them in the dishwasher. Bella wet a clean dishrag and handed it to Landon. "Hey, buddy. How about cleaning the syrup off the table?"

Landon snatched the cloth and did as instructed, then tossed it from the table into the sink. When it landed where he wanted, he shot both arms in the air. Then he turned and raced Livie to the bathroom.

Tucker leaned his back against the counter. "Woman, you promise them the world or something? Or worse, a puppy?"

She looked up from where she'd been wiping flour off the counter. "What? No, of course not. They didn't want to get out of bed, so I told them if they got up and got dressed like they were supposed to, then we could make very special pancakes for breakfast. And I added that they had to take care of their dishes when they were done."

He ran a hand over his tired face. "Well, it worked. You're good for them, *Izzie*."

She wrinkled her nose and wagged her finger. "No way, pal. Only the cutest twins on the planet get to call me that."

Livie and Landon ran from the bathroom, toothpaste caught in the corners of their mouths, shoved their lunch boxes in their backpacks hanging on low hooks in the laundry room, then Livie turned to Isabella. "Izzie, will you walk us to the bus today?"

Tucker pressed a hand to his chest and staggered back. "My heart. It's broken. My daughter has replaced me."

"Oh Daddy. You're silly. No one could replace you. I just want Izzie today."

He crouched in front of her. "And that's okay with me as long as she doesn't mind. Have a great day. Make good choices. And remember what?"

"You love me to the moon and back." She flung her arms around his neck.

"That's right." He gave her a hug and pressed a kiss to her fruit-scented hair. Then he turned to Landon, wrapping him in a hug. "Hey, my man. Same goes for you— have a great day and make good choices."

"I will, Dad. Love you."

"Love you, too, buddy."

As Bella headed out the door and through the garage with his kids, he watched from the kitchen window as the three of them stood together at the end of the driveway.

Like a family.

His children needed a woman's presence in their lives. Someone to make them special pancakes, guide them in cleaning up their messes and walk them to the bus.

Someone like Bella.

Stop that.

He could not let his heart sway his head.

As soon as Livie and Landon hurried onto the bus, Bella waited for it to head down the hill, then she turned and headed back to the house, her arms wrapped around herself.

She breezed in through the laundry room with the chill of the morning clinging to her. The rose-colored tip of her nose made him want to lean down and kiss it. Instead, he refilled his cup. "Thanks again for coming to our rescue last night. With Dad and Claudia out of town, I appreciated it even more."

"No problem. I'll finish cleaning up the breakfast mess and get out of your hair." She brushed past him and finished wiping off the counters. "There are leftover crepes. You can store them in the fridge and warm them in the microwave—cover them with a plate so the steam will heat them without drying them out."

He laid a hand on her arm. "You've done plenty. Leave the mess. I'll take care of it."

"No, you need sleep. I'll be done in just a few minutes, then you can have the place all to yourself—peace and quiet."

Problem was, he didn't want peace.

These days, he disliked the quiet.

"You learn to make crepes in culinary school?"

Bella shook her head, her hand stilling a moment. "No. My mother taught me. When I was about the twins' age, actually."

"Your mother? You don't talk about her."

She lifted a shoulder. "There's not a lot to tell. Dad and I weren't enough to make her stay. She went back to France when I was five, and I haven't heard from her since."

"France? Man, Bella. I've known you most of my life and I never knew your mother was from France. Is that why you enjoy French cooking so much?"

"I don't know. I guess part of me figured if I could excel at cooking and opened a cute little French bistro, make a name for myself, then my mother would find me worthy enough to have in her life. But apparently she has loftier goals than parenthood."

"What do you mean?"

"Have you heard of Solange Boucher?"

"Of course. Who hasn't? She's like the next Julia Child, or at least that's what someone mentioned when I caught one of her shows on the cooking channel."

"She's my mother." Spoken quietly, her words were edged with wistfulness and perhaps sadness.

Tucker's eyes widened. "What? Solange Boucher is your mother?"

Bella nodded, her eyes downcast as she scrubbed the same spot on the counter. "My dad met her when he was in the navy. His ship, a subtender that's since been decommissioned, had gone to the Bahamas for some offshore training exercises. My mother was there on holiday with her family. She and my dad met at a French patisserie, and he said it was love at first sight—for him, anyway. They wrote back and forth, and when he left the navy, he went to France and asked her to marry him. She accepted, and they had a small wedding in a park outside Paris. They both loved cooking and talked about opening a restaurant together. Dad said moving to the States and giving up everything she'd known was tough on her. I was born just after their first anniversary. When I was five, her father became very ill. She went back to France to see him and never returned. Apparently, it was more important for her to make a name for herself over there than to be here with her family in the States."

"I'm sorry, Bella." He touched her hand.

She shrugged. "It is what is it. My dad was devastated when she refused to come back. I had no contact with her after that. I don't know if that was her choice or his. All I know about my mother is what's shown in the media. I used to make her cards every Mother's Day, holding on to hope that one day she'd walk back through our door. But she never did."

"I can only imagine how painful that has been for you. I've always had family around, so it's hard to know what that would be like. It's been five years since Mom was killed, and there are times when I still want to call out for her when I walk into the farmhouse."

"How do we get over that? You're grieving for those you loved and lost, and I'm grieving for a woman whose life choices were more important than parenthood."

"Grief takes on many different forms, and it's not something you just get over. It takes time, and the process is different for everyone. You need to allow yourself to process it and learn how to move through it, but part of you will always cherish the time you had with the person you lost."

"Even after twenty-five years, I'm not so sure I've moved through it. Almost everything I do is based on her and hoping to be enough for her to want me back in her life. How pathetic is that—a grown woman still trying to make her mommy proud?" Bella sniffed and brushed a hand under her eyes.

"Bella. It's not pathetic at all. I don't think we ever get over losing a parent, no matter how old we are when it happens. My heart aches that Landon and Livie don't even remember Rayne. They know her from pictures and stories, which is why I try to keep her alive for them." He tipped up her chin. "But you understand that loss and being here with them gives me peace. And the fact that they love you, too."

Bella nodded as she rinsed out the dishcloth, then she gripped the edge of the sink. "I love being here."

That same wistful tone again.

He stood behind her and rested his hands on her shoulders. "Why do I sense there's a 'but' coming?"

"They're great kids, Tuck. You're very blessed. But this arrangement is only temporary." She turned and folded her arms over her chest. "The longer I'm here, the harder it's going to be to say goodbye."

His heart slipped in his chest.

"Goodbye? Going somewhere?"

Shaking her head, she sighed. "No, but with the diner reopening in a few days, I'm going to be swamped with helping Dad. I want to help you as much as I can, especially with all the help you've given with me, but—"

"But you're only one person with very little time. No worries. I get it. I knew this wasn't permanent. I appreciate all you've done for us."

"I'm not going to leave you in a lurch."

"Bella, my childcare issue is not your problem. Your concern is helping your dad. You've put in a long hours this past week, and I really appreciate what you've done for us. So well, by the way." Cupping her face, he stroked a thumb across her cheekbone, then slid a lock of hair behind her ear. Sliding a hand behind her neck, he pulled her to him gently and lowered his mouth to brush a kiss across her lips.

Bella sucked in a breath and took a step back, her eyes

wide. She touched her lips, then looked up at him with large golden eyes. "Y-you kissed me."

"Yes, I did."

"Why?"

"I don't know."

"Is this going to become a habit?"

"Do you want it to be?"

She pressed a hand to his chest and lowered her eyes. "I don't know. I don't want to be used, Tucker."

"Used? What are you talking about?" He frowned and took her hand in his.

She drew in a breath. "I'm totally fine with helping with the kids and appreciate the help you're giving me in return, but I won't be a stand-in because you're missing your wife."

"You think—" Tucker dropped her hand and turned away, grinding his jaw. Pulling in a deep breath, he exhaled slowly, then looked at her. "If my kiss offended you, I apologize. I kissed you because… I don't know. The way the sunshine coming in through the window highlighted your face. Or maybe the sweet look you gave me. Or maybe to help ease some of the pain you're still feeling. Or maybe I wanted to assure you that I see you. Not Rayne. But whatever. Again, I'm sorry. It won't happen again."

That was exactly why he needed to keep distance between his head and his heart. The last thing he wanted was to hurt Bella…or get hurt in return.

Chapter Six

Tucker had kissed her.

Tucker. Had. Kissed. Her.

And she'd ruined the tender moment by being a total jerk about it.

Oh, why did he have to go and complicate their relationship like that?

They were friends helping each other out. Nothing more.

Last night she'd tossed and turned with those same questions bouncing around in her head. Only to remember the gentleness of his lips against hers.

Oh, for crying out loud, she sounded like a sixteen-year-old. Next, she'd be doodling his name in her notebook.

Grow up.

It was just a kiss.

He was clear about not wanting to fall in love again, anyway.

And wasn't that what she wanted, too?

Her parents' marriage had proved love only led to heartbreak. Better to be a glorified nanny than to get her heart involved.

She needed to get her mind off Tucker and back on her work. She had a menu to finalize and specials to plan for the upcoming week.

Outside the rear kitchen door, high-pitched voices followed by low male tones grew louder, then the door opened and Livie and Landon burst into the kitchen.

"Izzie, we got you a surprise!" Livie and Landon thrust fistfuls of handpicked black-eyed Susans at her.

Isabella pulled off her gloves and tossed them in the trash. Smiling, she knelt in front of them and accepted their offerings. "Thank you. They're perfect. I love them."

"I picked mine first, then Landon copied me." Livie made a face at her brother.

"Did not."

"Did too."

"Guys, does it matter? Giving gifts and being kind isn't a competition." She smoothed Livie's flyaway hair back from her face. "I always wanted a brother or sister to copy."

"Why? It's so annoying." Livie's dramatic stretch of words and deep sigh made Isabella smile.

"Maybe Landon wants to be like you."

Landon wrinkled his nose and made gagging sounds. "Ew, gross. I don't want to be like a girl."

Behind them, Tucker burst into laughter, the rich sound causing Isabella's stomach to jump.

Oh, good grief.

Still holding the wilting bouquets, Isabella headed to the service station in the dining room to retrieve a drinking glass. She returned to the kitchen, filled the glass with water and added the flowers. Then she set them on the pass-through window. "Now I can see them while I work. What are you guys doing here? Hungry? Anyone want a snack?"

"We had to go to the dentist to get our teeth counted. Daddy bought us ice cream cones."

Isabella shot Tucker a look and raised her brow. "Ice cream and I wasn't invited?"

He had the good sense to look chagrined as he pulled a lidded paper cup with a red straw out from behind his back and handed it to her.

She took it and drew on the straw. Thick chocolatey sweetness chilled her mouth. "This is so good. I haven't had a chocolate shake in forever. Thanks for thinking of me."

"You're welcome. Remember how we used to stop by Sweeney's and get shakes after work on Saturdays?"

Taking another sip on the straw, she lowered her eyes and nodded. And chose not to remind him that their weekly shake dates stopped after he started dating Rayne. "I haven't thought of Sweeney's in years."

"They closed about eight years ago." Tucker took her hand, his fingers still cool from holding on to her milkshake, and squeezed. "I'm going to run the kids back to school, then I'll return and sample this special burger you've been talking about."

She glanced at his long, strong fingers with nicks and scars covering hers and nodded. "I'll be waiting."

Oh great. Now he'd think she was eagerly awaiting his return.

He grinned and herded the twins back outside amid their choruses of goodbyes.

Once they left, she donned another pair of gloves and moved to the six-burner to make her red wine vinegar aioli. She measured out vinegar, brown sugar, orange zest and a handful of seasonings and combined everything in a saucepan to boil. Then she let it simmer and reduce down before incorporating it into the mayonnaise.

Twenty minutes later, Tucker returned smelling of fresh air and sunshine. He rubbed his hands together. "Let's sample this burger."

After four years of culinary school and another six in one of the best kitchens on the East Coast, Isabella could handle a measly burger.

But this wasn't just any burger.

It was a make-it-or-break-it burger.

Or at least it seemed like it.

Why did cooking suddenly make her nervous?

Probably had something to do with Tucker leaning against the counter watching her every move.

And for now, she needed to leave it at that.

Dig any deeper and she'd be setting herself up for more heartache.

"What did you call this again?"

"The Liberty burger—I felt it went with Dad's All-Star theme. It's made with local grass-fed beef, red wine aioli, local bacon, Gouda cheese and caramelized onions. Scott, the executive chef at the Briarwood, who's dating my friend Sarah, suggested it—he said it was a French and American fusion to represent Lady Liberty being a gift from France."

"Very patriotic."

Isabella grabbed a metal spatula and flipped the hand-formed patty onto the toasted ciabatta roll. She criss-crossed two strips of bacon on top of the patty, added Gouda cheese and spooned a dollop of red wine aioli on a bed of caramelized onions resting on the open-faced roll. She layered lettuce and tomato, added the top of the bun, then speared it with a wooden pick. She placed the burger next to a side of baked sweet potato fries with maple-mustard dipping sauce. Grabbing her towel, she wiped the blue-rimmed plate, pulled off her gloves, tossed them in the trash, then set the plate on the prep station to snap a quick photo. After stowing her phone, she reached for the plate and turned to hand it to Tucker.

But before he could take it, a loud grinding sound from the hood—like pennies being chopped in a blender—startled her. As she whirled around to see what was happening, the plate slipped out of her hands and landed upside down at her feet. Maple mustard dripped off her shoes.

With a final grind and crackle, the noise stopped suddenly, leaving behind a stench of burned rubber. Her gaze swung between the smoking hood system and the ruined food on the floor.

The stress and exhaustion of the last two weeks pressed down on her, weighing like boulders on her shoulders. Her breath caught in her throat, and her chest rose and fell as the numbers for replacing the system raced through her head. The cost ratcheted the anxiety trembling through her.

Without a working hood system, they couldn't open.

If they didn't open, then they couldn't generate income to help pay off Dad's loan.

And if they didn't pay off Dad's loan, then they'd lose the diner.

Her chest shuddered as moisture wicked her brow.

Tucker gripped her arms gently. "Hey, everything's going to be okay."

She shook her head as her vision blurred. "No. No, it's not. How can you say that? We're ruined before we even had a chance to get started. We're supposed to re-open day after tomorrow, and the hood motor just blew."

"We'll get it fixed."

Isabella dragged her hands over her head. "It's going to cost several thousand to replace, and I'm tapped out,

Tuck. I drained my savings to help catch up Dad's loan and to pay for updating the dining room. He barely made payroll last month. The whole motor needs to be replaced, and it's illegal to run a kitchen without it. So, until we can get it replaced, we can't open. And if we don't open, we can't generate sales. It's a catch-22."

"Let me help."

"How? Are you an HVAC contractor in addition to your other skills?"

Tucker laughed. "No, I meant I can pay for it."

Isabella shook her head. "No. No way. I just said it's going to cost a couple grand to fix, at least."

Tucker reached for a napkin and used it to dry her cheeks. "Bella, let me help. That way you can be up and running in time for the reopening on Monday."

"You're so sweet, Tuck, to want to jump in and save people. But this isn't your fight."

"You sound so much like your dad, you know?"

Isabella shrugged. "What can I say?"

"Say yes." Tucker tipped up her chin. "Joe paid for my EMT training after Rayne and I got married. Did you know that?"

Isabella shook her head.

"At the time, I protested, but he said friends who were like family help each other out. So now, it's my turn. I'm a family-like friend who wants to help. Consider it a payback for everything your father's done for me and my family." He lowered his voice as his thumb stroked a stray tear off her cheek.

She turned her face into his palm, the warmth of his hand seeping into her skin. And for a second, she allowed herself to savor his touch. Coming home and being around Tucker...well, that stirred feelings in her chest that she'd buried long ago.

Or so she thought.

But now, being here with him, close enough to rest in his arms, she drew in a deep breath and slowly released Tucker's hand, taking a step back just outside the circle of personal space.

She grabbed a towel and crouched to clean up the broken plate and spilled food, careful not to catch one of the shards in her finger as Tucker's offer rolled around inside her head.

So tempting, but it wouldn't be right.

She dropped the towel in the trash.

"Bella—"

"I'm thinking, okay?"

"About what? How to tell me no?"

"Tuck, I appreciate the offer, but paramedics aren't rolling in dough. Plus, you're paying for tuition and you have a family to care for. How can you afford to loan us a couple grand for a burned-out motor?"

"I have money in savings."

She shook her head. "No. Definitely not. Forget it."

"Why?"

"You need that for your kids. Thank you, but I'll figure out something."

"You complain about your dad's pride, but you're as stubborn as he is."

"My dad—"

"Let me worry about Joe, okay?" Tucker stepped closer and cradled her face in his hands.

Her breath hitched in her chest as she searched Tucker's blue eyes, then dropped her gaze to his slightly parted lips. If she took one step toward him and lifted her chin about half an inch…

The back door swung open, bringing in the sounds of outside traffic.

Tucker dropped his hands and moved away from her. Dad carried in a box of produce and dropped it next to the prep sink. His gaze swung between the two of them. A frown puckered his forehead.

"Tucker."

"Joe."

Dad lifted his nose. "What smells like burned rubber?"

Isabella swallowed. Hard. Then twisted her hands. "Dad, don't freak out, okay? The hood motor just blew."

He strode over to the hood system and looked at it. Then he turned back to her and shrugged. "No big deal."

"What do you mean, no big deal? Without a working hood system, we can't cook. And with the reopening in a few days—"

Dad held up a hand. "Calm down, Bells. When they installed the new hood system a while back, I bought an extra motor to have on hand. I'll call Alena and see if one of her HVAC contractors can replace it before Monday."

Isabella closed her eyes and buried her face in her hands as relief whooshed through her.

Finally, something was going right. Maybe, just maybe, the reopening would go off without a hitch after all.

What if Tucker was wrong? What if he wasn't limited to only one happily-ever-after?

What if, like his dad and Claudia, he could get a second chance at a relationship?

Problem was, no one could replace Rayne. Not that he was looking for a replacement, but how did he go about dating someone new without comparing her to his late wife and what they'd had together?

If Joe hadn't walked in, Tucker would've kissed Bella.

Despite promising her just the day before that he wouldn't do it again.

Instead of terrifying him, though, the interruption frustrated him.

For the first time since Rayne died, another woman had gotten under his skin.

Bella, with her messy painting and incredible cooking, who had a way with his children. Which could mean only one thing—he was ready to move forward with someone new, someone like Bella.

Tucker leaned forward, elbows on his knees, and traced the fading tan line on his ring finger. He'd removed his wedding ring several months ago, but it wasn't until Bella returned to Shelby Lake that he'd even considered the possibility of more.

A fresh start.

He scrubbed a hand over his face and zeroed in on the frames lining the mantel.

But if he wanted to start fresh, he couldn't have photos of his late wife staring at them from every direction.

Pushing to his feet, Tucker blew out a breath, took a couple of steps forward, then reached for one of their framed wedding portraits. Rayne, with her white-gold hair wound in a fancy updo—or whatever she called it—around a delicate tiara and dressed in a white gown that had stuttered his breath in his chest, stared at him through the glass. The smiling couple had made promises for eternity, not realizing their happily-ever-after would be so short-lived.

He traced the curves of her face as heat pricked the backs of his eyes. "I loved you, you know. Losing you… man, that was rough. For all of us. One of the hardest things I had to go through. As much as I wish you were here, I can't live in the past. It's time to move on, Rayne. For the twins' sake. And for mine."

He ran a thumb under his wet eyes and reached for a layer of bubble wrap, enfolding the frame in the plastic, then stood it upright in a box he'd retrieved from the attic.

He'd put smaller pictures of their mother in the twins' rooms so they wouldn't forget her. When they were older, they could choose what to do with the others.

He reached for the eleven-by-fourteen family photo that had been taken when Olivia and Landon were six weeks old.

The doorbell rang, causing Meno to bark and race from the room. Still holding the picture, Tucker followed him and opened the door to find Bella standing on the welcome mat holding a takeout container. His heart jammed against his ribs.

Dressed in skinny jeans, ankle boots and an ivory sweater and puffy red vest, she looked much more collected than she had a couple of hours ago.

He rested his forearm against the doorjamb. "Hey."

"Hey, yourself. Can I come in?"

He shrugged and took a step back. "Sure. Yeah."

Bella walked past him, wreathing him in a scent of vanilla. "I made you another burger."

"Did you get the hood system fixed already?"

"Not yet, but Dad has someone coming to replace it. I cooked this upstairs in our kitchen. It's best eaten hot, but hopefully you can still get an idea of what I'd like to have on the menu." She handed him the box.

Setting the frame on the table near the front door, he opened the container and lifted the bun. "What did you say was on this again?"

"Grass-fed beef, bacon, Gouda cheese, caramelized

onions, red wine vinegar aioli, lettuce and tomato on a toasted ciabatta roll."

"Pretty fancy burger."

Isabella lifted a shoulder. "Not really. Just wanted to change things up a bit."

"Don't change too much. Joe's customers like what he's offering."

"Well, the menu can use more fresh vegetables and salads."

He peered at the lettuce and tomato on the burger, then shot her a smirk. "You mean, more than the toppings on this burger, right?"

She nudged him. "In addition to this burger, I mean."

Tucker set the container on the table and pulled out a chair and gestured for her to sit. He sat across from her and picked up the burger. "Let's see what we've got."

He bit into the sandwich, absorbing the tang of the aioli mingling with the sweetness of the onions and the crispness of the lettuce. He grinned around the food. "Good beef."

"Really?" Bella, who had been sitting on the edge of her chair, slumped against the wooden back.

He swallowed the bite and reached for a napkin out of the holder in the middle of the table. "Yes, really. I think it's going to be a winner. Grass-fed beef, though…that's going to be a pricey burger."

"I'm trying to pull in locally sourced meats. Hopefully, Dad's customers will appreciate that and won't mind paying a little more to help their neighbors."

"You have a compassionate heart, Bella."

"I'm just trying to show Dad's investment in the community." She glanced at the frame on the table. "That's the picture from the living room, isn't it?"

"Yes. I'm trying to decide whether to put it in Olivia's room or Landon's."

"Why?"

Tucker pushed away the plate with the half-eaten burger and folded his arms on the table. "Because it's time. As much as I loved my wife, I can't move forward if her pictures are all through the house. I don't want Olivia and Landon to forget her and it's getting easier to share stories, so I'll put her pictures in their rooms and save some for when they're older."

Bella reached for his hand and gave it a gentle squeeze. "I'm sorry you had to suffer such a great loss. You two were a perfect match."

Tucker looked at her long fingers with trimmed, un-polished nails. His gaze shifted to her face and the empathy rimming her eyes, then he chuckled and leaned back in his chair, slowly removing his fingers from her gentle touch. And regretting it instantly. He rubbed a hand over his chin. "You know, you kind of had something to do with us getting together."

"Me? How so?"

"Remember that Sadie Hawkins dance our junior class did as a fund-raiser?"

"Yes. Rayne asked you to attend, and then the two of you started dating afterward."

"Yeah, well, I'd been hoping you were going to ask me. I dropped hints and even asked who you planned to take."

Bella looked at him with wide eyes. "Really? You would've gone if I'd asked you?"

"Definitely. But when you didn't and Rayne did... well, I guess—"

"The rest is history."

"Something like that."

"I knew Rayne liked you and wanted to ask you to the dance."

"You did?"

She nodded. "During our class play, I was her stand-in. She told me."

"So you backed off."

"I figured she had a better chance with you than I did. But everything happens for a reason, right?" She shot him an overly bright smile, then lifted the family portrait off the table, her words bouncing against the glass. "I mean, if you and Rayne hadn't gotten together, then you wouldn't have Livie and Landon."

"When I married Rayne, I expected us to grow old together. I'm thankful for our years together and, of course, Olivia and Landon. Now, though, it's time to move forward. Again, I have you to thank." He took the frame from her and set it on the table, turning it facedown.

"Me? What did I do?"

"You came home. Being around you helped me to see it's time to lay the past to rest and begin a new chapter in my life. If your dad hadn't walked in earlier at the diner, I would have kissed you."

Pink blushed her cheeks as Bella looked away. "Like I said yesterday, I don't want to be anyone's stand-in. Rayne takes up room in your heart. There's nothing left for anyone else."

Even though her words had been spoken softly, Tucker felt as if he'd been slapped. He moved out of his chair and stood beside her, pulling her to her feet. He lifted a hand and cupped her cheek, his thumb caressing the softness of her skin. "Bella, you aren't anyone's stand-in. While I will always love Rayne and cherish our years together, I'm not looking for a replacement."

She covered his hand with her own. "I got burned

badly last year when the guy I was dating used me as a rebound after ending a long-term relationship. I guess it still stings."

"You don't deserve to be treated that way."

Shrugging, she gave him a smile that didn't quite reach her eyes, pulled her hand away, then stepped back. "Yeah, well, that's life. I don't want to take up any more of your time, but I wanted you to try the burger."

He glanced at the half-finished burger and smiled. "Thanks. It's great, and I think it's going to be a hit. The diner's really coming together, Bella. You've been working hard."

"Just trying to help my dad hold on to his dream."

"What about you? What do you want?"

She cast a look over his shoulder, then crossed her arms over her chest and lifted a shoulder. "For years it's always been having my own kitchen. A small, upscale restaurant that still captures the heart and soul of the foods I love to cook—comfort foods with fine dining. I'd call it Bella's Bistro. But now, I just don't know anymore."

"Why not?"

"Priorities shift, and dreams change. I used a chunk of my savings to help Dad. And quite honestly, I'm not even sure he appreciates it. He's been so grumpy and growly since I've been home, I'm ready to pack up and leave. Problem is, without a job or a place to live, my options are a bit limited. Sometimes I feel a bit stuck."

He understood that.

"I hope you don't leave. I, for one, will miss you if you do. And Olivia and Landon will, too."

Her shoulders sagged as she leaned against the table and rubbed her eyes. "I'm tired, Tuck. And scared. What if this doesn't work? What if it doesn't turn the diner around? What if Dad loses the business?"

"Your dad's a lot tougher than you may think. And God doesn't give us a spirit of fear. He gives us courage and power and love and a sound mind to make good choices. You are strong and courageous, Bella. And so is your dad. You've been working so hard and just need some downtime. It will help with your perspective."

"I can't. Too much to do."

"What would you do if you had the day off?"

She sighed and smiled. "A morning stroll through the farmers market, a bike ride around the lake before it gets too cold, snuggling in a blanket around a campfire while watching the stars. But that won't be happening for a while, if at all. Like I said, there's just too much to do."

Tucker took a step toward her and lifted her chin. "There's always going to be too much to do. You need the downtime, so take the day and do all of those things. With me."

A frown creased her forehead as her eyes tangled with his. "W-with you? And the twins, you mean?"

"No. You and me."

She pulled her gaze away and let out a slow breath. Then she nodded and gave him a slow smile. "Okay."

The single word, spoken barely above a whisper, had him wanting to fist pump the air, but he pocketed his hands and smiled. "Great. How about first thing in the morning? We'll start with the farmers market."

She nodded and reached for the doorknob. "Great. See you then. I have to get back to the diner."

Tucker reached over her, opened the door and held it open as she stepped outside and strode down the walk. Once she reached her car, she gave him a quick wave, climbed into her car and backed out of the driveway.

Pressing his back against the doorjamb, he waited until she headed down the hill and disappeared out of sight.

What would it take for him to convince Isabella she was an original, the lead in her own story?

And was he truly ready to take that next step? To be the one to show her she wasn't anyone's stand-in? Especially his late wife's?

For the first time in years, he felt something he wasn't sure he'd feel again.

Hope.

And he wanted to hold on to it as long as he could.

Chapter Seven

If Isabella could turn back time, she'd go back a dozen years and give her teenage self a head slap.

If she'd asked Tucker to the Sadie Hawkins dance all those years ago, would they have started dating and maybe ended up married with a family?

So hard to say.

But she had been too scared to put herself out there.

Now she wasn't going to allow herself to speculate on what could have been. Tucker had chosen Rayne. And Isabella had chosen her culinary career.

Leaving Shelby Lake had helped her get over seeing Tucker and Rayne together every day. But now that she was back, she spent more and more time thinking about Tucker.

Did he mean it when he said he was ready to move forward?

The man hadn't dated anyone since his wife's passing.

Was he truly ready?

If she didn't stop thinking about Tucker, she was going to drive herself crazy. She needed to focus on things within her control. Like getting the rest of the hometown heroes' photos hung on the diner's all-star wall.

She hung the final framed photograph of one of Shelby Lake's enlisted servicemen, a Marine Corps corporal serving in the Middle East, and smothered a yawn. As she stepped off the small ladder, the front door opened.

She turned to find Tucker holding the door for his stepmom, Claudia, and his future sister-in-law, Tori, who was also Claudia's niece.

Isabella lifted a hand, shooting Tucker a puzzled look. "Hey, guys. What's up?"

"Hey, Bella. Sorry for showing up unannounced, but Claudia and Tori brought Olivia and Landon home after you left. I told them about that awesome burger and, well… Tori wanted to talk to you."

"Sure." She glanced between Tori and Claudia, who were dressed nearly alike in jeans, brown knee boots and long cardigan sweaters with patterned scarves wound around their necks. She was thankful she'd decided not to change out of her clothes after leaving Tucker's and waved a hand toward one of the empty booths. "Have a seat."

Instead of complying, Tori trailed her fingers over the freshly painted walls and ran her hands over the booths Dad had installed that morning before the hood system blew, wreaking havoc on her emotions. She straightened a new placemat menu on one of the round tables down the center of the dining room, and then she stopped in front of the all-star heroes' wall, resting an elbow on a ladder rung as she gazed at the framed photos lining the wall.

Smiling, Tori turned around and headed back to the booth, sliding in next to her aunt. "Isabella, you have a gift. This diner looks amazing. You've created a warm, homey feel that's going to draw in plenty of customers." She opened her purse, pulled out a card and handed it to

Isabella. "I work for a PR firm, and I'd love to help the diner with advertising."

Isabella took it and glanced at the card before pocketing it for later. "I really appreciate that, Tori, and I'm sure Dad would, too, but our budget is a bit tight right now. Would any of you like something to drink?"

Claudia held up a hand and shook her head. "Thanks, but I'm fine."

Tori slid in next to her aunt and looked at Isabella, folding her hands on the table. "Every time I talk to Livie and Landon, they tell me about the wonderful food you make together when you're caring for them. And after hearing Tucker rave about your cooking, Jake and I wondered if you'd be willing to cater our upcoming wedding in May."

"Are you serious?" Isabella jerked her gaze between Tori, Claudia and Tucker, who shrugged and shot her a smile that tripped her pulse.

"Yes, but we aren't having a big wedding. Just family and close friends. I'm sure you're used to much bigger venues."

"Actually, um, I don't have a lot of solo catering experience. I've done events at the resort where I used to work, but I haven't coordinated anything on my own. Are you sure you want to hire me?"

"I have plenty of experience coordinating events, but our guests do not want to be subjected to my cooking. If you think you could handle an event with about fifty people, we'd love to talk numbers and menus with you."

They talked for about ten more minutes about menus, courses and possible budgets. Then Claudia and Tori stood and headed for the door with Tucker trailing behind. He turned and gave her another heart-tossing grin. "Thanks, Bella. Again, I'm sorry for just dropping in."

She grabbed his hand. "No, Tucker, thank *you*."

Later that evening, with her conversation with Claudia and Tori still swirling in her head, Isabella spooned cranberry-apple-balsamic reduction over the roasted Cajun pork tenderloin she removed from the oven. She sliced the meat and rested it on top of a bed of rice-quinoa blend alongside roasted asparagus with a cranberry compote. She wiped the edge of the plate with her towel and carried it into the living room, where Dad sat in his recliner watching a game on TV.

"Okay, Dad, here's the third entrée I'm considering to go along with the roasted chicken and beef tips. Tell me what you think. If you like it, maybe we could add it as a weekly special or something."

With his focus still on the TV, Dad took the plate and cut a piece of meat without commenting on the presentation. Isabella tried not to stare while he spiked a stalk of asparagus and bit into it.

His lack of comments did little to stop the gymnastics in her stomach.

He finished half the meal without a word, and Isabella couldn't stand it for another second. "Well? What do you think?"

Dad reached for the remote and muted the TV. The sudden silence unnerved her. He set the half-finished food on his side table cluttered with fishing magazines, pill bottles and a cold cup of coffee. "It's good."

Good? That's it? She hadn't spent the last four hours in the kitchen for *good*.

"Okay, then. Thanks." She walked behind the recliner to take his plate.

"Hold up." He wrapped a hand around her wrist. "I'm not done eating or speaking."

"Sorry." Isabella set the plate back on the table, then

moved to the plaid couch that had sat in the same spot for the past twenty-five years. She stretched out her legs and pulled out her phone to thumb through her favorite chefs' social media feeds in an effort to appear nonchalant about her father's comments.

"Bells, there's no denying you're a talented chef, and the food is good. More than good. It's great, actually. But, sweetheart, you're trying too hard. Shelby Lake isn't like the Briarwood clientele. Sure, we have some classy folks, but most people around here are looking for comfort food. And I'm good with that. So, before you present Jake and Tori with a fine-dining menu and budget that will cause their eyes to pop, dial it down a little. You can make wonderful homemade meals without breaking the bank." Dad finished his meal, then set the plate back on the table and reached for the remote.

As the sounds of the coaches' whistles and sports commentary filled the room, Isabella stared at her phone, digesting his words.

She'd spent years taking criticism on her cooking, often constructive, but sometimes comments tore at her ego. While she'd always valued her father's opinion, tonight she'd hoped for a little more enthusiasm.

Why was she trying to be something more than what she truly was? She was the greasy spoon girl, the one who fit nicely in the friend zone, the one who didn't rock the boat, the one who needed to stay in her lane.

Problem was—she wanted more, but how did she go about getting it? The more time she spent in Shelby Lake, the longer she'd stay a hungry chef, unfulfilled with achieving her destiny, her purpose.

Maybe Tucker was right—maybe it wasn't up to her to make sure her father held on to his dreams.

But did she truly have the courage to embrace her own?

Even if it meant leaving everything she was growing to love?

No, the problem was, despite what her head said, her heart longed for more—the love and partnership that only came from a loving spouse.

But that meant trusting someone else to be there for her. Could she risk putting her heart out there only to have it trampled and bruised? Could she handle being abandoned one more time to figure out how to deal with the rejection all by herself?

But what if Tucker was right?

What if she did look to the future and put her trust in God? Could He have a future for someone like her? Was she willing to risk it to find out? But what if He turned His back on her, too?

Then what?

Did she have the courage to at least try?

Tucker was fine.

At least that's what he kept telling himself.

Maybe, just maybe, if he kept repeating it enough times, people would begin to believe him. And maybe he'd believe it, too.

Until then, he kept moving forward, because any other direction dropped him to his knees with memories that slammed him in the gut.

Three years since he'd gotten the call that shattered his world. Three years since the love of his life died a senseless death from something she'd ingested and reacted to. The anaphylaxis had happened so quickly, there hadn't even been time to make it to the ER. Three years since he'd struggled to figure out a new kind of normal.

So, yeah, he needed a night like this—Friday evening at the farmhouse surrounded by the love and laughter of family, brainstorming wedding plans over homemade pizza.

Needing some air and quiet after helping his dad and Jake clean up the kitchen, Tucker stepped out onto the front porch with Meno at his heels and sat in one of the Amish-made hickory rocking chairs Dad had gifted Claudia as a wedding present and clasped his hands behind his head.

Nightfall shrouded the fields to an inky darkness as a scatter of stars lit up the sky. The evening breeze whisked across his face, sending a chill down the back of his unbuttoned flannel over his short-sleeved T-shirt, and stirred dry leaves that had fallen on the porch. Cows bawled from the barn as they settled in for the night. Meno rested his chin on Tucker's worn leather slippers.

The front door opened, and Dad stepped out carrying two steaming cups of coffee. He handed one to Tucker then settled in the other rocking chair. "Figured you could use something to warm you up in this cool air."

"Thanks, Pops."

"What's going on?"

"Just listening to the sounds of the animals settling in for the night."

"Something else on your mind?"

"Why do you ask?"

"You seem a little distracted tonight. Wondered if maybe your thoughts were hanging out at the bottom of the hill."

"Maybe. At least partially." Tucker leaned forward and pulled a folded envelope out of his back pocket, handing it to his father. "This came today. I got in."

Being able to say the words out loud filled him with a sense of satisfaction he hadn't expected.

Dad took the cream-colored envelope and pulled out

the letter. He retrieved his reading glasses from his front shirt pocket, set them on his nose, then lifted the paper to catch enough light from inside the house to read the print.

Tucker pulled out his phone and flicked on the flashlight, then handed it to his dad. "Here, Pops, use this."

Dad took the phone and held it over the paper.

A couple of minutes later, he grinned and folded the letter, handing it back to Tucker along with his phone. "Way to go, Tuck. I knew you could do it. Why didn't you say something sooner?"

"I didn't want to horn in on Jake and Tori's excitement about the wedding."

"You always did put others first. Still, this is worth celebrating."

"I'm not sure if I'm accepting yet or not."

"Why not? You've been working hard with the online classes to get your gen ed credits so you can transfer onto main campus."

"I've spent the last three years trying to figure out how to pick up the pieces of my own life. It just seems so crazy right now with work, caring for the kids, keeping the house from turning into an episode of *Hoarders*, helping on the farm. Plus, it's an hour commute each way. I've thought about putting classes on hold until we get settled into a better routine."

"It's going to be an adjustment, for sure, but wouldn't being on main campus give you more focused time for your degree?"

"Yes, and I've been thinking about that since the letter arrived. Doing classes online is convenient for family and work, but there are constant distractions. This is my first semester, and there are days when I wonder if I'll even make it to finals in December. Having Bella around to help with my kids has been a huge boost."

"But is she planning to stick around? Joe seems to think she's only home for a short while."

"I'm not sure she and Joe are on the same wavelength. She wants to help him with the diner, but she hasn't said how long she plans to stay. She seems to be at loose ends right now."

"I'd hate to see you get hurt, son."

"I'll be fine."

"Mind if I ask you a question?"

"Shoot."

"Why do you want to become a grief counselor, Tuck? You're a gifted paramedic."

Tucker focused on a stain on the porch left by a wet leaf that had since dried and blown away. How did he answer Dad's question without sounding like an idiot?

The rocker creaked as Dad stood and placed a hand on his shoulder, giving it a gentle squeeze. "Do you suppose you could be searching for a way to work through your own grief? After the tornado killed your mom and nearly destroyed the rest of us, then Rayne's death, that was a triple whammy for you. But you just kept going. And today's the anniversary of Rayne's death. Have you even allowed yourself to grieve properly?"

Easing out of the chair, Tucker stood and stuffed his hands in the pockets of his jeans as he focused on the silhouette of the fence in the field across the road. "I had to keep going. When I lost Rayne, I still had babies to care for. We're Holland strong, remember? That's what we do." He waved a hand over the property. "With the farm nearly rebuilt, you marrying Claudia and Jake and Tori getting married, we're good. Everything's good. I'm fine."

If that were true, then why did he still have that hollow ache in his chest?

Dad moved in front of him. The interior lights cast a glow on the front porch and offered enough light for Tucker to see the concern in his father's eyes. "Are you? Really? For the past couple of years, you've been in survival mode. And yes, your life is a bit chaotic right now as you're trying to move forward without Rayne. I've been there—I had to learn to live again without your mother. I'm telling you—it's the hardest thing I've ever done."

"I told you I'm fine." He winced against the sharp edge of his tone and softened his voice. "Thank you for your concern. I appreciate you looking out for me. And the way you help with Livie and Landon. Truly. I'm not wallowing in misery. I'm going into work—even covering shifts for my coworkers. I'm pushing through classes even on days when I'm dog tired and want nothing more than a warm bed and a soft pillow. Olivia and Landon are fed, clothed and thriving. We're fine. I'm fine."

Dad considered him a moment, then nodded, although the frown between his eyes and the creased forehead stayed in place. He clapped him on the shoulder. "Since everything's just fine, then you shouldn't defer enrollment. Life's only going to get harder from here on out, so grab onto this opportunity while you can. Claudia and I are here to do whatever we can to help you."

Tucker pulled his father into a hug and battled the unexpected wetness clouding his vision. His chest tightened, and he cleared his throat. "Thanks, Pops. I appreciate it. More than you know."

Without another word, Dad let go of him and headed back inside, leaving Tucker alone in the darkness.

He *was* fine.

Just fine.

He had to be.

Because falling apart wasn't an option.

He had too much at stake.

And since Bella had come home and walked back into his life, he had someone he trusted to help care for his children. That had to be something, right?

Problem was, so many of those buried feelings had been working their way to the surface the more time he spent with her. As his heart waged war with his head, he battled wanting to cling to the memories of the love he lost and making new memories with the one who had gotten away.

Chapter Eight

They were going as friends, right?

No reason to think otherwise.

So how did one dress for a friend date?

A cute wear-one-last-time-before-cold-weather-sets-in dress would be fine for walking around the farmers market, but not so much for biking around the lake.

Isabella stared at the growing pile of clothes on her bed and the last few hanging in her closet.

Ugh, this was so ridiculous. *Just pick something already.* She was a grown woman, not some giddy fifteen-year-old going on her first date.

No wonder she felt more comfortable in her chef whites. With a clean, pressed uniform, hair pulled back and her toque in place, she didn't have to worry about impressing anyone with her appearance…and falling short. Instead, she dazzled with her cooking skills.

Today, though, that was a different story.

This is ridiculous. Tucker didn't care what she wore— after all, they were just friends.

Tired of the insecurity, she pulled a yellow-and-white-striped tunic over her head, slipped into a pair of fitted jeans, wrapped a white infinity scarf around her neck and grabbed a denim jacket for later. She slid her feet into her favorite tan ankle boots and zipped up the sides.

After securing her hair in a messy bun, she shouldered her purse and headed for the car.

It would have to be good enough.

Five minutes later, she scored a parking spot not far from the market. She scoured the rows of vehicles, searching for Tucker's silver SUV, but she couldn't see it.

Maybe he was running late.

With a couple of string market bags tucked in her purse, Isabella strolled to the nearest vendor to wait.

The Briggs' Bee's Knees booth offered bottles of honey for sale as well as other honey-based products like lip balms and moisturizers. She was in the middle of listening about the importance of preserving honeybees when her cell phone rang.

"Excuse me." She fished her phone out of her back pocket and saw Tucker's face appear on the screen. "Hello?"

"Hey, where are you? I've been at your door for the last ten minutes, but everything's locked up and no one is answering."

"My door? I thought we were meeting at the farmers market."

"Why would you think that?"

"Well, because you asked if I wanted to go, and I said yes."

"Right. And when a guy asks a girl to go someplace with him, he usually picks her up."

Oh.

So maybe this was a date.

She gripped her stomach. "Sorry. Want me to head back?"

"No, I'll meet you there, then we can decide what to

do about your car when we're done at the market. See you in five."

"Okay." She stayed on the fringes of the park so she could see Tucker when he arrived. She didn't want to waste any more of their day together with her own stupidity.

Within minutes, Tucker pulled up behind her car and strode across the lawn wearing faded jeans, a light blue V-neck T-shirt and gray sneakers. With the slight breeze toying with the waves in his hair and his dark sunglasses, he looked like he'd walked off a photo shoot.

And she wasn't the only woman admiring him, either.

Man, the guy knew everyone. His name had been called at least ten times in the short span from the sidewalk to where she waited.

He reached her, a wide smile highlighting his face, and wrapped her in a one-armed hug. "Hey, you. You look terrific."

"You're only saying that because I'm your friend." She smiled up at him and breathed in the scent of his body wash coiling around her.

He looked at her with…hurt in his eyes? He frowned and shook his head. "Bella, why would you doubt my words? If I say something, I mean it."

"Sorry."

Oh man. This day was going to be harder than she'd imagined. She wasn't so great at small talk. "And I apologize for the confusion. If you can't tell by now, I don't do a lot of dating."

"We're together now, right? And for the record, I haven't had a first date in fifteen years."

She nodded and fell in step with him as they moved to one of the fruit vendors lifting boxes of apples off the back of his truck.

"Look at the size of those apples." Breathing in the sweetness of the fruit, Isabella reached into a bushel basket and grabbed a large yellow Ginger Gold at the same time Tucker did. His warm hand covered hers. She let go of the apple and pulled her hand away. "Sorry."

"For what?"

She shrugged, hating the way her face blazed. Why did she have to be so socially awkward?

They wandered through the rows of vendors selling fresh herbs, organic produce, farm-fresh eggs and locally sourced meats.

"You know, if the community garden takes off, your family could consider having a booth at the market next summer."

"Maybe. I know there are a lot of new regulations, so we'd have to look into those. Has your dad mentioned anything about overseeing the garden?"

Isabella shook her head. "I don't know what's going on with him. He's just not himself."

"You know, diabetes can create problems with more than blood sugar. It affects a person's mental health, too. Diabetes distress causes mood swings, depression and anxiety. Joe's been in control of his world for so long that not being able to manage his blood sugar may leave him feeling a bit powerless. Being a proud man, he won't ask for help."

"I feel helpless not knowing what I can do to help him."

"Just talk to him. Remind him you're there to listen, not judge. Offer to take a walk with him. Ask if he wants you to go to his appointments and hear what his doctor has to say."

Isabella laughed. "Have you met my dad? He'll shoot me down with all of those."

"Be patient. Once his medications start working, you'll see the same ole Joe returning. And in the meantime, I'm always here if you need someone to talk to." Tucker brushed the backs of his fingers across her cheek.

She captured his hand and squeezed. "Thanks. What would I do without you?"

"Maybe we don't have to find out."

Before she had a chance to process what he'd said, Tucker glanced at his watch. "You ready for the next part of our day? I called this morning, and the bike rental at the lake is still open. We can see if they have any left."

"Sure, let's go."

As they crossed the park, a female voice called his name. "Tucker!"

He turned, and a bright smile lit up his face. He held out his arms as a petite brunette ran into them and wrapped her arms around his neck. He dropped a kiss on her cheek and stared down at her. "So great to see you! What are you doing here? When did you get back?"

"I got in last night. I wanted to pick up a few things from the farmers market, then I was going to call you later this afternoon. I wasn't quite sure of your work schedule."

"I'm off today. In fact, Bella and I were about to head to the lake." With an arm still wrapped around the woman's shoulders, Tucker turned toward Isabella. "Sorry. Bella, meet Willow, my sister-in-law. Willow, this is Isabella Bradley. Her dad owns Joe's All-Star Diner at the bottom of the hill."

Willow stepped away from Tucker and held out her hand. "You went to school with Rayne and Tucker, didn't you? You guys worked together at your dad's place."

"That's right. Bella's a classically trained chef, but she's just helping her father out for now."

She was probably reading more into Tucker's words, but did he feel like she was settling by helping her father? Like it was a step down for her?

"Oh, that's great to hear. I love Joe's." Willow turned back to Tucker. "Hey, listen. I'd love to see my niece and nephew. I've missed them terribly. Maybe tomorrow?"

"You know, that may work out well. My nanny quit, so Bella's been helping me out. But now that the diner's about to reopen, your timing couldn't be more perfect. Right, Bella?"

All she could do was smile and nod. And try to repress the rope of jealousy coiling within her.

"Yay." Willow clapped her hands the way Olivia did when things went her way. "I gotta run, but I will stop by later to get Meno. Great seeing you, and meeting you, Isabella."

Isabella smiled and lifted her hand in a small wave.

"Man, talk about perfect timing, right?"

Perfect for Tucker, maybe.

She'd known all along their arrangement was temporary, but she hadn't expected to be dropped so quickly. They'd planned to bake cookies tomorrow before bed. With Tucker's birthday coming up, she'd wanted to do something to celebrate him, especially since he went out of his way for everyone else.

But now it didn't seem like she'd get the chance.

As they drove to the lake, Tucker carried most of the conversation, sharing mostly about Willow.

At the lake, they parked in the gravel lot beside a weathered red building advertising bike rentals. Tucker paid for two bikes, then shrugged on a bulging backpack before making sure she was ready to take off.

Seagulls dipped and soared over the water as Tucker and Isabella strapped on their helmets and pedaled down the asphalt path rimming the water. Rays of sunlight burst through long branches laden with changing leaves, stripping the crimson to a pale peach and casting shadows over the path. Gentle waves splashed against the shore. Fresh air tinged with a hint of wet earth and fish breezed over her. Sunshine warmed her face, and Isabella should have been soaking up the relaxing atmosphere.

Instead, her brain continued to rewind Willow flying into Tucker's arms.

They'd ridden for about a mile, reaching the park at the end of the trail. Tucker's phone rang, and he braked to answer it. She pedaled over to the edge of the fountain to give him some privacy.

Three little boys close to the twins' ages played tag between two sturdy oak trees as two women sat on a bench chatting and watching them. An older couple walked a small, white dog that stopped to bark at the boys.

After ending his call, he rode over to her and jerked his head back to the bike trail. "Follow me."

Tucker pulled over into the grass, parked his bike under a shady poplar tree turning a golden yellow and waited for her. "Hey, slowpoke, what's taking so long?"

Once she parked her bike next to his, he waved a hand toward the tree. "Care to join me for a picnic?"

After unzipping his backpack, he shook out a rolled-up blanket and spread it out in the shade of the tree, then pulled out a couple of water bottles and a crumpled, oversize paper lunch bag with foil-wrapped packages sticking out.

Isabella sat on the edge of the blanket and pulled her knees to her chest.

"You're being quiet. What's going on?"

What could she say? She was jealous of the way he

hugged Willow? Or her quickness to take over caring for the twins, essentially pushing her out of the picture?

"Nothing. I'm good."

He eyed her. "Why don't I believe you? What gives?"

She picked up a fallen leaf and twirled it between her thumb and forefinger. "I know they're not my kids or anything, and I don't have any say about it, but I'm disappointed we won't have our last couple of days together. I totally get Willow caring for them was the plan all along. I'm just disappointed, that's all."

"I'm sorry. I didn't stop to ask how you felt about it. I was so surprised to see Willow and didn't give her suggestion a thought other than it would help you out. Forgive me?"

He looked at her with such sincerity in his blue eyes that she wanted to smooth down the curls being tagged by the lakeside breezes. Instead she nodded and jerked her chin toward his backpack. "Of course. Now I hope you plan to feed me after that ride."

"Most definitely." Tucker reached inside the bag and handed her a foil-wrapped packages. "Before I met you at the farmer's market, I stopped and grabbed carnitas tacos from Lena's food truck. They're much better hot, but I'm sure they'll still hit the spot. And listen, if you would like to watch the kids as planned, I'll let Willow know. I'm sorry for deciding on your behalf."

"It's fine, Tuck. You make the choice. Just know I'm here if you need me."

Tucker raised an eyebrow as a slow smile slid across his face. "Oh, there's no *if* about it, Bella. I definitely need you. You're a good friend."

Her insides quivered as she unwrapped her tacos.

Of course, he meant he needed her to help care for his

children. Because they were *friends*. Reading anything else into it would only lead to heartache.

Tucker could get used to evenings spent around a crackling campfire with his family and listening to his kids' laughter as they raced under a black sky scraped with stars.

Not to mention having a beautiful woman sitting next to him, tucked in one of his sweatshirts.

Bella, Tori and Claudia chatted about menus for the upcoming wedding. Tucker glanced at his brother to find Jake watching his fiancée with a grin, bringing joy to his face.

Long overdue joy.

Tucker gave Jake's foot a little kick. "Hey, man. I wish it was bright enough to take a picture of that cheeseball grin on your face."

"You're just jealous of my good looks."

"Yeah, that must be it." Dad stood slowly and jerked his head toward the farmhouse. "You boys mind giving me a hand with the s'mores stuff?"

"Not at all, Pops." Tucker pushed to his feet, but before he followed his dad and his brother, he turned to Bella. "I'm heading into the house. Need another drink? You warm enough?"

She pulled her attention away from Tori and Claudia and, nodding, she reached for his hand, giving it a quick squeeze. "I'm fine, thanks."

Tucker pulled his hand away from hers reluctantly and hurried to the back deck, taking the steps two at a time.

In the kitchen, Dad and Jake leaned against the counter, arms folded and grins creasing their faces.

"What's going on?"

"You tell us."

"Tell you what?"

"You and Isabella seem to be hitting it off."

"We've known each other since kindergarten. Of course we're hitting it off."

"But it's more than that, isn't it?"

"I don't know, Jake. Maybe once I sort out my feelings and jot them down at my journal, I can let you read it."

Jake held up both hands. "Whoa, man. I was just bustin' on ya. No need to be a jerk."

Tucker scraped a hand over his face. "Sorry."

Dad clapped a hand on his shoulder. "You like her."

It wasn't a question but a statement spoken by a man who understood what it meant to lose his first love and be offered a second chance at happiness.

He nodded.

"Have you told her?"

"Not yet."

"Why not?"

Tucker shrugged. "Timing just doesn't feel right."

"Maybe she thinks you see her only as a friend."

"Well, that's partially true—she is my friend. When you started dating Claudia, did you feel like you were cheating on Mom?"

Dad pulled out a chair, the wood scraping against the ceramic tile, and straddled it.

"No. Your mother is gone, and nothing is going to bring her back. She was the light of my life, and I'll always cherish the memories we made together, but I can't live in the past. Neither can you. You'll know when it's time to pocket the memories you've made and move forward."

"Thanks, Dad."

"You're welcome." Dad handed the boxes of graham crackers to Jake and tossed the marshmallows to Tucker.

He grabbed the basket with chocolate bars and peanut butter cups and headed out the door.

"How many men does it take to carry out stuff for s'mores?" Claudia teased as she took the basket from Dad.

"Is this where I wait for the punchline?" Dad tilted her chin and dropped a kiss on her lips. "We were having some father-son bonding time."

"We wondered if you were sneaking the chocolate." Tori stood and wrapped her arms around Jake's waist.

"No need to sneak when we can have it freely." He unwrapped a peanut butter cup and popped it in her mouth.

Several months ago, Jake had been the one struggling with his relationship with Tori. Now seeing them together gave Tucker hope for his own future.

If Tucker wanted more, then he needed to be willing to take the first steps in moving forward. So, what was holding him back?

Bella knelt on the grass near the fire between Livie and Landon as she guided them in toasting their marshmallows. She listened intently as they talked and helped turn their long handled forks so the flames wouldn't devour their marshmallows.

Yes, he could fall for Isabella Bradley very easily.

He just needed to make sure they were ready. All of them. Because the last thing he wanted was to hurt those he cared about.

Tori stuck a marshmallow on her fork and sat on her haunches next to Bella. "What's it like working at a place like the Briarwood? It must be exciting to make meals for all of the famous people who come through there."

"It's an upscale vacation resort near the Adirondack Mountains in New York. I didn't see them, since I spent most of my time in the kitchen, but the servers used to tell us stories." She sandwiched Livie's marshmallow between two graham crackers and pulled it off the fork.

"How long have you worked for them?"

Bella's cheeks reddened as she rubbed sugary residue off her fingers. "Actually, I don't work there anymore."

"Oh, Bella." Tori rested a hand on her arm. "I'm sorry for being nosy."

"Don't be. I got blamed for something I didn't do and lost my job, which is why I came back home."

"And the silver lining was you found your dad on the diner floor. If you hadn't lost your job and come home, only God knows what could have happened to Joe."

Bella returned to her chair, slipped the hood of her sweatshirt on her head and burrowed deeper into the hoodie as if she were trying to become invisible. The pinched lines around her mouth and the disappearing spark in her eyes made him think there was something more than what she was saying. Not that she had to share anything with any of them, but the last thing he wanted was for his family to make her feel uncomfortable. Especially since he hoped she'd be around a lot more.

Tucker touched Bella's shoulder. "Hey, wanna go for a walk?"

She nodded.

He looked at his dad and jerked his head toward Livie and Landon sharing a chair and happily eating s'mores. "Pops, mind keeping an eye on the hooligans for a few minutes?"

"Nope, we've got them."

Bella shoved her hands in the pockets of her borrowed hoodie. "Tucker, there's something I need to tell you."

"First, I'm sorry if Tori made you uncomfortable."

She shook her head. "No, not at all. She was simply curious. But that's kind of what I want to talk to you about. I've never really said why I came back home, and you haven't asked."

"I figured you'd tell me when you were ready."

She raked her fingers through her hair. "Here's the thing—I got fired because of a cross-contamination issue. I made desserts for a wedding and one of the bridesmaids was hospitalized for reacting to peanuts, but I know the pastry kitchen was spotless when I started baking. I knew one of the bridesmaids was allergic to peanuts and made special effort to ensure there were no peanuts in the area. I ended up losing my job. After I left, they learned one of the new busboys had spilled peanut flour and tried to clean it up without anyone suspecting anything. Some peanut dust managed to get on tarts I had made and the bridesmaid had eaten. I'm allergic to shellfish, so I'm always very careful."

"Wow, Bella. That really stinks. You couldn't fight for your job back?"

"After the humiliation of losing my job and walking out in front of the kitchen staff, I just couldn't go back. Then I came home and found out what's going on with Dad and the diner, so I've been here."

"Would it be horrible of me to say I'm glad you got fired?"

"Why would you be happy about that? I loved my job."

He threaded his fingers through hers. "Because it brought you home—and back into my life."

Chapter Nine

If Isabella could take a mental picture and frame it, she'd title it *The Essence of Family*, because helping Tucker rake leaves for Olivia and Landon to jump on was one of those memories that deserved to be captured and savored time and time again.

The twins had come up to her after church and asked her to join them for lunch. A quick look at Tucker showed his approval, so Isabella hurried home to change, then arrived at their house to eat sloppy joes before heading outside.

And it was worth it to hear the twins' laughter and to see them playing so well together.

White-gold sunshine streamed through the blackish-gray branches of the sturdy maple tree in the front yard and spotlighted the twins jumping in the piles of purple, citrus and scarlet leaves Tucker had been raking for the past hour.

Even Meno wanted in on the action, digging his nose in the pile and following Livie and Landon as they took turns jumping.

Tucker leaned on his rake and watched the activity. "Maybe if they jump long enough, they'll wear themselves out and want naps. Then I can get some studying done before I need to leave for work."

"Want me to take them for a bit so you can study?"

"Nah, that's not necessary. I'm sure you have a bunch of stuff to do for tomorrow. Besides, Willow is keeping them tonight."

Maybe she should have come up with an excuse to say no to lunch. The more time she spent with the Hollands, the more she wanted to be a part of their family, and that wasn't going to happen.

She'd have to put some distance between them eventually, so it was probably a good idea Willow was going to be caring for them.

"Bury me, Livie." Landon fell back into the leaf pile and flung out his arms.

Olivia scooped up armfuls of leaves and showered them over him. Instead of burying him, she dropped beside him and moved her arms and legs. "Look, Daddy. Look, Izzie. I'm making a leaf angel."

"And a beautiful one at that." Isabella pulled out her phone and snapped a few pictures of the twins and Tucker.

"Daddy, what's that?"

Tucker followed the direction of Livie's finger.

A small black-and-white animal ran into the cut cornfield across the road, then suddenly, it went down with a yelp.

"You two stay here." Tucker dropped the rake in the grass, then hurried across the road. He crouched at the edge of the field.

Isabella crouched beside him and pressed a hand against his back. "What do you see?"

"I think it's a dog. Maybe it's lost. Or maybe it was dropped off and abandoned by its owner."

"That makes me so sad."

"It's not uncommon. We've seen it countless times living up here on the hill."

At the sound of their voices, the animal lifted its head, showing a black face with a white muzzle, neck and eyebrows. With its ears pinned back, the dog looked at them with wide, sad eyes.

"Would you go into the house and get some of Meno's food and some water? Maybe we can get the dog to come closer. I'm going to give Willow a call and see what we should do."

"Willow? Why?"

"Oh, didn't I tell you? She's a licensed vet." He reached for his phone at the same time as the dog took a step closer. Tucker held out his hand.

"Be careful. We don't know where it came from or if it has rabies."

His lips curled up. "I've been handling animals since I was Landon's age."

"Right." She pushed to her feet and jogged back across the road. She guided Livie and Landon to give her a hand in the house with getting some food and water.

A few minutes later, they stayed in the yard while she took the bowls to Tucker, then shrugged off her hoodie and handed it to him. "Maybe you can wrap it in this."

He smiled his thanks. Still crouched, he edged closer to the dog, talking to it in a soothing voice.

The dog lifted its head and sniffed. It moved closer to the bowl.

Tucker moved a little closer but stopped when the hair on the back of the dog's neck rose. He pushed the bowl closer to the dog, then waited.

The dog eyed them, then sniffed at the bowl. It tested

the contents with its tongue, then put its nose in the bowl and devoured the food.

"I don't see a collar or any identification tags, but with the laceration across the dog's nose and its dirty, matted hair, it's most likely a stray. I'm suspecting with its protruding belly, this dog could be pregnant."

"What do you want to do?"

"Get her in the house and give her a quick exam. I tried to call Willow, but she didn't answer. I left a voice mail. She has access to a microchip scanner in her office, so she can help us identify the owner if the dog is chipped." Tucker held out his hand, and the animal crept closer to investigate.

They took turns talking to the animal in soothing voices. When it moved close enough for Tucker to touch, he patted the dog's shoulder.

The dog trembled, and Tucker pulled his hand away. "You're scared, aren't you?"

Finally, the dog allowed Tucker to pick her up and wrap her in Isabella's hoodie. "Hey, would you mind carrying her into the house while I grab the rakes and my medical bag from the car?"

Tucker transferred the animal into Isabella's arms. The dog whimpered, and Isabella talked to her as they crossed the road.

Tucker retrieved the rakes and carried them into the garage, then retrieved his medical bag. Isabella followed Livie, Landon and Meno into the kitchen. "Where do you want me to put her?"

He nodded to the counter. "Set her up here so I can get a good look."

"Daddy, can we see the doggie?" Livie danced around in excited circles.

"No, baby, this doggie is scared. I want you and Lando to keep your distance for now."

"But we won't hurt it."

He rested a hand on her head and smiled at her. "I know you won't, but the doggie doesn't know that and could hurt you without meaning to. You can watch me check her over, but no touching. Got it?"

They nodded and hurried to the dining room table to grab chairs.

Feeling the dog's trembling increasing, Isabella cradled it closer to her chest. Tucker helped the twins move chairs to the counter and stood between them to examine the dog while Isabella held on to her.

Tucker touched the dog's abdomen gently. "I'm guessing this dog's going to be a mama within the next month or so. She'll need an ultrasound to be sure, but in all the years we've had dogs, her size suggests she's more than halfway through her pregnancy. Let's get her bathed and warm. Then she can rest." He left the kitchen then returned with a bottle of baby shampoo.

"What will you do with a litter of puppies?"

"There's no way I can keep them. I can barely handle Livie and Landon. To add puppies to the mix would be a recipe for disaster." Tucker ran warm water into the sink and laid another towel on the bottom. "Zoe Sullivan, who runs Canine Companions, takes in rescue dogs. Let's try to find her owner first. If no one claims her, then we'll get in touch with Zoe about helping us to find her a forever home."

The way Tucker kept using the plural, like they were partners in this venture, filled Isabella with an emotion she couldn't quite name.

"Daddy, can we watch a show?"

He glanced at the clock above the kitchen sink and

herded them off the chairs, returning them to the table. "One show, then we'll talk about dinner."

They followed Tucker into the living room. A moment later, laughter sounded from the TV.

After rinsing the shampoo out of the dog's coat, Isabella sat on the kitchen floor, wrapped her in a towel and rubbed her dry. The dog curled up in Isabella's lap and sighed.

She totally understood that sigh, that need to find a place of safety, of belonging.

"You two look content." Tucker sat next to her and wrapped his arms around knees drawn to his chest.

"I know you're right—neither of us can handle a litter of puppies—but this dog needs someone to love her, someone to help her heal and feel whole again, someone to watch over her as her pregnancy progresses."

"What are you thinking?"

"If an owner doesn't claim her, I'd like to take her. Maybe for Dad. He has such a gentle spirit despite his recent gruffness, and I think Dory could be a great support dog for him. He could get exercise by walking her and have company in the evenings after the diner closes."

"Dory, huh?"

She shrugged. "Well, you have a Meno. Dory just seemed to fit. I don't know. I just think she was sent to us for a reason. I know you have a lot on your plate right now, but if Willow can get her checked and see about an owner, then I can help with expenses and care for her, since it doesn't look like I'm going anywhere soon."

He looked at her, his blue eyes softening. "I'm liking the sound of that." He leaned over and brushed a kiss across her lips. "You have a tender heart, Bella."

She could get used to kissing Tucker. But then that

would lead her to wanting more than what either of them was ready to offer. Staying friends kept her safe from heartache.

Isabella wasn't a quitter and she wasn't about to start now, but if she continued at this rapid pace, she'd be toast by lunch.

She'd keep it together and prove she could handle whatever was tossed her way. And if this morning was anything to go by, they had nothing to lose. Their breakfast rush packed the place with a line out the door.

Isabella scanned the wheel for the new tickets Kathy and Dana had added. "Okay, we have two strawberry crepes, a spinach and mushroom omelet, and two eggs over easy."

"Spinach and mushroom? Since when is that on the menu?" George, who'd been cooking at the diner since Isabella was a child, scowled at her.

"Since we updated the menus to offer some healthier options."

The older man with grizzled hair and a thin build scowled and waved a spatula. "What was wrong with the old menu? Too many changes will drive away the customers. Mark my words."

"George, I love you like an uncle, but you need to trust me."

"And you gotta trust me. I've been cooking in this diner for twenty years. I know what the people want."

"According to the reviews I've been reading online, some people want more than greasy burgers and onion rings."

"Then they can get that someplace else."

"That kind of attitude is why the business is failing.

If we don't change, people will find other places to eat. Then what?"

"Why do you care?"

"This is my dad's diner. I don't want to see it close."

"Then maybe you shouldn't have waited so long to come back home." He untied his apron and tossed it on the food service counter. "Since you seem to know more than me, I'm done. Handle it yourself, young lady."

George's words knifed her, flaying her open. The rear door opened and slammed shut.

With her face the same temp as the flat top, she bit down on the words clawing to be free and ladled her homemade crepe batter into a heated skillet. She cracked two eggs into a metal bowl, beat them with a little more force than necessary and poured them onto the sizzling flat top. She added a handful of chopped spinach and sliced mushrooms, then folded it in half.

She flipped the crepe in the pan, then turned it over on a plate. After adding a spoonful of sliced strawberries, a dusting of powdered sugar and a spray of whipped cream, she set the plate on the pass bar. A couple of seconds later, the omelet joined the order. She rang the bell, alerting Kathy and Dana to their orders, then scanned the new tickets.

How did Dad handle this six days a week for the past twenty-five years? She'd worked in fast-paced kitchens for years, but always with a team. None of this solo business. No wonder he was worn out.

She pulled in a deep breath and focused on the ticket Kathy pinned to the wheel. "This one's for Bernie at the counter."

"Who's Bernie?"

"Retired schoolteacher who comes in the same time

every day, orders the same breakfast and sits in the same spot."

Isabella skimmed the ticket. Two eggs, two sausage links, whole wheat toast.

Easy enough.

She had the breakfast prepared and placed on the pass bar in less than five minutes.

Kathy returned a moment later and set the plate on the pass bar. "You forgot his chicken broth."

"Chicken broth? For what? I didn't see that on the ticket."

"Joe's put a spoon of chicken broth over Bernie's eggs every day for the last ten years. It's such a habit that I don't think about it."

Isabella's eyes whizzed across her station as she searched for the chicken broth. She finally found some in the reach-in, opened it and heated it in order to spoon some over Bernie's eggs.

Kathy smiled her thanks and took the eggs away.

For the next hour, Isabella hustled getting orders out in a timely manner. Soon breakfast service would end, then the lunch crowd would descend, wanting their meals quickly so they could get back to work.

She reached above the flat top for a plate, but her fingers touched a bare shelf.

She'd been so busy manning the orders that she hadn't noticed the sounds from the dishwashing station—or lack thereof.

"Dana, who's our dishwasher?"

Her head bent, she shrugged. "Don't know. Louis quit. Not sure who Joe hired to replace him."

"Quit? When?"

"Just before your dad ended up in the hospital. They

had a blowup in the kitchen, and he walked out. Joe said he was going to hire someone new."

One more thing he'd neglected to tell her. Was he trying to fail on purpose?

Isabella scanned the tickets, then eyed the growing pile of bus pans. She hurried over to the station, scraped plates and racked them in a tray to push through the dishwasher.

She rushed back to the grill and worked through the tickets, alternating getting plates out and catching up the dish area.

The back door to the kitchen opened, bringing in a rush of traffic sounds.

Isabella glanced over her shoulder to find Tucker carrying a beautiful bouquet of autumn-colored flowers.

The sight of him scrambled her insides.

He reached her and touched her cheek. "Happy Grand Re-opening Day, Chef."

His words sent a rush of tears to her eyes. She blinked them back and forced a smile. "Thank you. They're beautiful. Not to sound rude and ungrateful, but you shouldn't be back here, and I don't have time to chat."

He shot her a look she couldn't read. Or couldn't take the brainpower to process.

"No problem. I'll carry these to the dining room." Tucker pushed through the swinging kitchen door.

Isabella tried to pay attention to the brioche French toast to prevent it from burning, but the sound of Tucker's laughter in the dining room challenged her focus.

He returned to the kitchen with a scowl on his face. "Why are you running this kitchen by yourself?"

"George walked out. Apparently, the dishwasher quit before the diner closed and a new one hasn't been hired. Dad hasn't made an appearance."

"That's not like Joe."

"I know, but I can't get away from the kitchen long enough to check on him."

"I'll head upstairs and see what's going on, then I'll come back down to give you a hand."

Isabella needed to remind him he wasn't allowed in the kitchen unless he was an employee, but the truth was, she didn't care about rules right now. She was just relieved to have an extra pair of hands.

Tucker returned a few minutes later, a dark expression on his face. "Your dad's in the shower now. He'll be down shortly."

"What's going on?"

"Says he overslept."

"Dad's been awake at five every day for as long as I can remember."

"I'm thinking it was more like a pity party with a solo guest. Your dad's been dealing with a lot lately, and I'm sure all of the changes have him a bit rattled. He didn't know George walked out, leaving you on your own."

"So I'm drowning down here while he's feeling sorry for himself? He's not the only one dealing with changes."

Tucker stood behind her and gave her arms a gentle squeeze. "I know. Let me pray for you, then I'll give you a hand until Joe comes down."

Isabella closed her eyes as Tucker's murmured prayer washed over her. He concluded the prayer with an amen.

"Thank you for coming to my rescue once again, but you should be home sleeping."

"Are you concerned about me?"

"I don't want you in your sleep-deprived state lopping off a finger and messing up my kitchen."

"Man, Bella, more sweet talk like that, and you're going to have me falling for you."

"We know that's not going to happen."

"Don't be so sure."

The quiet tone of his voice caused her hand to still. Her eyes jerked to his face, finding all joking replaced with a serious expression.

Oh no...

Surely, he just messing with her. Because anything else was too much to accept right now.

Chapter Ten

Despite the shower he'd taken before leaving the station, the acrid scent of smoke hung in his memory, coupled with the screams of the young mother who'd fought against treatment to find her child. Thankfully, the firefighters located him, but the woman's anguished cries at losing her husband in the blaze echoed in his ears.

Tucker pulled into the driveway, and the motion light above the garage activated, but the rest of the house remained shadowed and silent.

No glow in the windows welcoming him home. No one to talk with, to decompress from the tragedy that had struck their community.

With the twins staying at the farm tonight due to Tucker getting called out to help with a house fire, the place would be quiet.

Too quiet.

Maybe he could catch up on some homework. Or grab some necessary sleep.

He headed into the laundry room, wishing he'd at least remembered to leave the light above the stove on.

Rustling sounded in the kitchen. Probably Meno, who

it seemed wasn't going back to Willow's, or maybe Dory trying to get her bearings.

He felt along the wall for the light switch in the kitchen and flicked it on.

"Surprise!"

Tucker jerked back, tripping over his own feet, and smashed his elbow against the doorjamb. Pain lanced his arm as his heartbeat thundered in his ears.

Dad, Claudia, Jake, Tori, Bella, Livie and Landon wore ridiculous emoji party hats. Red, yellow and green balloons had been taped all over the walls—apparently the twins' decorating. Streamers trailed from the overhead light to the dining room table filled with a cake, bowls of popcorn, chips and M&M's.

Livie and Landon ran over to him, jumping up and down while clapping their hands. "Did we surprise you, Daddy? Did we? Were you surprised?"

Tucker knelt and wrapped an arm around each one of them and then lifted them up in his arms, careful to keep the points of their party hats from poking him in the eyes. "Yes, I am. What's all of this?" He looked over the twins' heads, his eyes locking with Bella's, who raised an eyebrow and shot him with a smile that nearly singed his insides.

"It's your birfday party, Daddy." Livie put a paper hat on his head.

"Aren't I too old for parties?"

Landon shook his head. "Nope. You're never too old. That's what Izzie told us."

"Is that right?"

With the twins still in his arms, he crossed the room to the table to find a homemade chocolate cake with thirty-two candles sitting next to emoji plates.

His eyes tangled with Bella's.

She saw past his jokes. Fought to tear down his wall. Saw a need. And filled it.

He wanted to exchange the twins to have her in his arms.

Olivia threw her arms around Tucker's neck. "Did you like your surprise, Daddy?"

"I sure did, punkin. Was this your idea?"

"Nope, it was Izzie's. You need to give her a hug."

"Is that right?" Tucker set Olivia down and looked at Bella. "I have you to thank for this?"

She shrugged. "You give to everyone else. You deserve to be celebrated."

He reached for her. The moment his arms wrapped around her and the warmth of her touch flowed through him, he relaxed. He tightened his hold and wove his fingers through her hair.

"Thank you," he muttered against her neck, his voice graveled and thready.

She pulled back and looked at him with concern. "You okay?"

"Rough day. A husband and young father died in a fire tonight trying to save his child."

"How awful. So sorry." She held him close and pressed a kiss against his jawbone.

For a moment, he stood there, allowing the heat of her embrace to seep into the cracks and crevices rocked apart by the injustice in the world.

Behind them, Dad cleared him throat. Bella dropped her arms and stepped back, her face brightening to a light shade of pink.

At the twins' insistence, she lit the candles. Then after everyone sang to him, Livie and Landon helped blow out the candles and reminded him not to share his wish or else it wouldn't come true.

As Bella sliced cake and scooped ice cream, he longed to confess his wish had come true—he'd found someone who had stolen his heart. Problem was, he wanted to be the one to claim hers. With her belief that falling in love only led to heartbreak, he just needed to take his time.

Nearly two hours later, close to ten, everyone else had left, leaving Tucker and Bella to get the sugar-infused bouncing kids settled into their beds. They'd insisted Izzie be the one to read stories, listen to their prayers and then shut off their lights. After kissing them goodnight, Tucker had headed for the living room.

Tucker wanted to curl up in bed, too, but he still had an hour or two of homework. Stretched on the couch with his closed laptop on his chest, he closed his eyes and exhaled.

This pace was getting old, and he was in only his first year of school.

How was he going to keep this up?

"Hey, you okay?"

He opened his eyes to find Bella sitting on the edge of the coffee table, her eyes full of concern.

"Just tired."

"And I tossed in a surprise party to add to your crazy day. I'm sorry."

He reached for her hand. "No, don't be sorry. What you did was so sweet."

"I hope you don't mind. Claudia said you don't really celebrate your birthday."

"I just didn't want to make a big deal of that day."

"Why not?"

Tucker sat up and turned to sit on the edge of the couch and scrubbed a hand over his face. "Because I didn't want to upset my parents."

"How would that upset them?"

He blew out a breath and lifted a shoulder. "When

I was nine, Mom got pregnant unexpectedly—a little girl. She was so excited, especially with four wild boys running in and out and trashing the house all the time. She spent the morning of my tenth birthday baking my favorite cake, blowing up balloons and decorating for my party that afternoon. After taping a banner on the wall, she had a sharp pain, lost her balance and fell off the chair. She and I were the only ones at home, and we didn't have a cell service up here at the time. I called 911. Dad came home from the store with my brothers as the paramedics pulled in."

"I can only imagine what he thought when he saw them." Bella moved off the table and sat next to him on the couch.

Tucker reached for his glass of water and took a drink. "Yeah, he was little freaked out."

"What happened with your mom?"

"Dad got in touch with my grandparents, and they stayed with us. I overhead Grandma crying and telling Grandpa they'd lost the baby. We canceled my party, and while everyone else was busy, I took down the decorations. Dad brought Mom home and put her to bed. I could hear her sobs through the heating vents in the ceiling. Dad knew I was upset about the party, but he told me I needed to be strong for Mom. Truth was, I was feeling really guilty. After seeing my mom like that, I begged one of the paramedics to save her. He promised to do his best. But then Mom was so upset about losing the baby. From that day on, I kind of stopped making a big deal since because I didn't want to remind my mom of the day she lost the daughter she wanted so badly."

"I'm so sorry."

Seeing the sadness on her face, Tucker wanted to wrap

her in his arms, but he stayed where he was. "It is what it is."

"How did your parents handle your birthdays after that?"

"Every year, they asked if I wanted a party, and I said no. Mom made my favorite meal and a cake. We kept the celebration low-key because I will never forget hearing her crying over what she'd lost."

"But what about you? You deserve to be celebrated. Of course, losing a baby is always traumatic, but your parents were thrilled to have you. What about your brothers? Did they have parties?"

Tucker nodded.

"Oh, Tuck." She placed a hand on his arm.

He glanced at her fingers, then at her face free of makeup with a freshly washed glow that made him want to reach out and touch it.

"I need to get going so you can get some sleep." She stood and jerked her head toward the hall.

He pushed to his feet. "Not yet. I have some work to do."

Bella frowned as they walked out of the room. "But it's late and you've had a long day."

"Unfortunately, my professors won't accept that as an excuse."

"You're off tomorrow. Can you do it then?"

"Yes, some, but I have a birthday dinner with my family tomorrow evening. Would you like to come?"

"You don't need an outsider at your family dinner."

"Outsider? Hardly." Tucker traced the line of her face. "I'd love to have you there."

She looked at him, then dropped her gaze to her fingers. She bit the edge of her lips and swallowed. "What are we doing?"

"Talking?"

"You know what I mean."

He took a step toward her and brushed his knuckles over her cheekbone. "What do you think?"

She cupped his hand and pulled it away from her face, but she didn't release it.

"Tuck, I…" She blew out a breath and took a step back. "I don't, I mean, well, the thing is…"

"No, I get it. I'm rushing you. I'm sorry. I'd still like you to come to dinner, but I'll understand if you choose not to." He placed his hands on her shoulders and pressed a gentle kiss to her forehead. "Thank you for the party. You're so great. I really appreciate it. And you. Now go home and get some sleep."

Bella pressed a hand to his chest. "Sleep well."

Not likely.

She slipped out the front door and closed it behind her, the click solidifying the barrier between them.

He returned to the living room and dropped on the couch, thunking his head against the padded back cushion.

Idiot.

What had he expected? She'd rush into his arms?

Despite her generous heart and responding to his kisses, she was his friend, and that seemed to be where she was content to stay.

But the more he was around her, the more he realized he was ready to move forward with his life, to have a relationship with someone who didn't seem to mind the package deal. He longed for a real marriage. He would always treasure their friendship, but his feelings were changing, and he was finding it harder to keep his distance.

But she wasn't ready.

He had no choice but to wait, no matter how long it

took. Somehow, he needed to gain control of his feelings. Otherwise, he was going to risk losing her before he could show her how perfect they could be together.

The noise around the table burrowed deep into Isabella's chest, imprinting a lasting memory. With nearly finished plates pushed away, serving bowls that appeared barely touched and the smells of sage, homemade bread and roasted chicken lingering in the air, Isabella appreciated being a guest at Tucker's birthday dinner.

Despite his desire to keep his birthday low-key, it was apparent how much his family loved him.

With her family being just her and her dad, being a part of tonight's celebration fed a need she hadn't even realized she carried until she sat next to Tucker and took his hand while Chuck prayed over the meal and the son he obviously cherished.

And he wasn't the only one.

Seeing Tucker dressed in tan khakis and an olive-colored pullover sweater over a white button-down shirt, her traitorous heart stumbled in her chest.

After everyone had finished the birthday apple crumb pie Tucker had requested, Livie and Landon crawled onto Chuck's lap, one on each knee, and they were laughing at something he'd spoken low in their ears. Livie lifted his coffee mug and took a sip before turning her face up to him with an impish grin.

The look of pure love and joy on Chuck's face— something that authentic just couldn't be faked. But then again, Chuck didn't have a phony bone in his body. No, he was the real deal, who knew how to love well and laugh often.

Did Tucker realize what a treasure he had with his family?

"Izzie, what do you call a sleeping cow?" Landon laughed between words.

Looking at Landon, she smiled and shrugged. "I don't know. Tell me."

"A bulldozer." Throwing himself against Chuck's chest, he collapsed into another fit of giggles.

Raising a brow, Tucker looked at his dad. "Recycling the old jokes, Pops?"

Chuck shrugged and grinned. "It's a new generation to appreciate my humor."

Across the table, Jake cleared his throat. "I know this is Tucker's night and I don't wish to take away from that, but Tori and I have some news to share."

He took Tori's hand and looked at her with such love that it pinched Bella's heart.

Would she have that someday?

Was it her imagination, or had Tucker put some distance between them since yesterday? Sure, he continued to laugh and joke with everyone else, but his tone changed with her, still friendly, but not as flirty as he was last night.

"We learned yesterday that Tori's sister, Kendra, and her niece, Annabeth, will be here in a couple of weeks for Thanksgiving. With Evan and maybe Micah coming home for the holidays, we've decided to move up the date of the wedding. Instead of getting married in May, we're getting married in two weeks. I know this doesn't give us a lot of time, but quite frankly, we don't want to wait. We want a very small wedding with only family and close friends. Evan's already agreed to stick around to help with the milking so Tori and I can get away for a honeymoon."

While the family rallied around the happy couple passing out hugs and good-natured ribbing, Isabella pasted a smile in place, but she felt out of place with the new celebration.

Part of her wished she could slip out quietly, but she didn't want to hurt Tucker's feelings. The more time she spent with him, the harder it was to disguise the truth—she was falling in love with her best friend.

While he was kind and generous and attentive and she knew he cared for her, she would never have claim to his whole heart the way Rayne had. And that filled her with a sadness that threatened to overtake her.

She wanted more than what her parents had had—a real marriage based on love and trust. Problem was, she wasn't sure how to let go of her mistrust and take a chance on having a future with someone she loved.

After hugging the couple, Isabella reached for dirty dishes and headed for the kitchen. She set the delicate china on the counter and ran water into the sink.

Outside the kitchen window, light snow dusted the ground and sugared the tips of the trees, turning the countryside into a holiday card.

"Are you planning to tell my stepson that you're in love with him?"

Jumping at the sound of Claudia's quiet voice behind her, Isabella flicked off the water and reached for a dish towel. "What? I… I mean—" She dropped her chin to her chest and sighed. Shaking her head, she looked at Tucker's stepmother. "Please don't tell him."

"Oh, sweetheart, of course not." Claudia crossed the room and enveloped Isabella in her warm vanilla-scented embrace. "I'm not the one he needs to hear it from. But can I say I know what you're going through?"

"You do? How so?"

"I don't know how much you know about Chuck and me, but Lilly, his late wife, was my best friend. My husband, who had cancer, had been gone for only a year when Chuck and I got married. Neither of us planned to fall in love—it was just one of those things that happened. For a while, I worried I would never claim Chuck's heart the way Lilly had, but then he reminded me, our romance was different than what he'd had with Lilly and I needed to focus on that. Just like Chuck will always love Lilly, I'll always love my Dennis, but I can still love Chuck with my whole heart."

Isabella folded a towel and placed it on the bottom of the sink before she started washing the delicate china. "I don't want to be a stand-in for Rayne."

"Do you really think he'd do that?"

"I keep telling myself Tucker's not like that, but I'm not very lovable. My own mother walked out when I was five."

Claudia grazed her fingers across Isabella's cheek. "Are you kidding me? God loves you completely and unconditionally. He created you and sent His son to die for you—that's the most beautiful definition of love. You are His daughter. I know it's so hard to trust when we don't know what the future holds, but that's what He wants—our unconditional love and trust, no matter what. Keep trusting Him, and everything will work out."

She longed to grab onto those words about trusting God and hold them against her chest. But what if she ended up getting hurt?

"How do you know?"

With her back pressed against the counter, Claudia grabbed a clean dish towel and picked up one of the plates. A shadow passed over her eyes. "Because I've had to trust Him over and over, especially after I lost my best friend when Tucker's mother was killed in that devastating tornado. And again when my sweet Dennis was diagnosed with cancer and passed away. Despite what we're going through, God's still in control, with a specific plan for each of us. When we go through those dark valleys, we can't always see the light, but all we have to do is look up."

She waved a hand toward the noisy dining room. "That family has suffered numerous losses, but they're getting their second chances at life and love. I've known Tucker since the day he was born. He's good and kind, but that boy has a stubborn streak. No one forces him to do anything. He invited you to a family event because you're special to him. If that doesn't tell you something, I'm not sure what else to say. Trust God, rely on Him even when it doesn't make sense and everything will work out in His perfect timing. That's how our faith grows and we become stronger. I promise."

"Bella."

She turned to find Tucker standing in the kitchen doorway. He cleared his throat and tossed his phone from hand to hand. "Sorry to interrupt, but I need to get Livie and Landon home and into bed. Would you like to join us, or…?"

His voice trailed off, giving her an out if she chose to take it.

She glanced at Claudia, who winked at her and pressed a hand over her heart before walking out of the room, leaving them alone. "I want to say yes, but with Jake and Tori's news, I need to get a jump start on the catering plans for their wedding."

He shoved his hands in his pockets and nodded. "Yeah, I get it. I think Jake's kind of tired of baching it. Not that I can blame him. Maybe we Hollands weren't cut out for the single life."

She wasn't loving the single life so much anymore,

either, but she didn't want to rush into a relationship because she was feeling lonely. Or vice versa. But if Claudia's words were to be believed and what she knew about Tucker was true, he was the real deal. He didn't believe in playing games. So maybe he was looking to be more than friends. And now it was up to her to decide if she was willing to trust him with her heart.

Chapter Eleven

It was a beautiful day for a wedding.

Despite the brush of snow across the fields and a brisk wind that turned a man's spine to ice, the weather forecast promised midmorning sunshine to help warm up the chill.

His breath visible in the air, Tucker shoved his hands in his pockets and bounced from foot to foot as he waited outside the barn for Bella to arrive.

The side door opened, and Jake stepped out dressed in faded jeans, a gray T-shirt and an unbuttoned blue-and-gray flannel untucked with the sleeves rolled up to the elbows. He pulled sunglasses out of his front pocket and set them on his face. "Hey, brother. What are you doing out here?"

"I'm waiting for Bella to help her get things set up. Shouldn't you be at the farmhouse making yourself pretty for your bride?"

Jake laughed and glanced down at his jeans. "Tori's stressing about the barn and decorations, so I promised to check and make sure everything was still standing."

"Well, after that windstorm collapsed the other barn

before the Fatigues to Farming fund-raiser, you can't really blame her."

"True. But she has nothing to fear today. Everything's going to be perfect."

"No doubt. With Tori's mad coordinating skills and Bella's amazing food, it's going to be a great day. I'm happy for you, man." Tucker thumped him on the back.

"Thanks, little brother." Jake's phone chimed. He pulled it out of his back pocket, read the words and a slow smile spread across his face as he typed back a reply.

For a moment, a pang of jealously snaked through Tucker, but he was quick to shut that down.

Jake and Tori deserved their second chance.

His brother waved his phone. "Evan just landed. He'll be here in less than an hour."

"Great. No word from Micah?"

Jake shook his head. "No, nothing. Not since he bailed during Dad and Claudia's reception."

"Don't be so hard on him, Jake. Micah's been dealing with stuff."

"And he chooses to go it alone. He's one of the reasons we started this Fatigues to Farming program—to give injured veterans like Micah a sense of hope." Jake scrubbed a hand over his face. "I can't think about that right now. I won't let anything ruin this day for Tori, including my own attitude. I need to head back to the farmhouse. I'll see you in a bit."

Jake strode across the parking lot and headed down the road toward the farmhouse, hands in his pockets and whistling.

When was the last time Tucker heard his brother whistle?

Yep, Tori was the best thing to happen to his brother in a long time.

Several hours later, Tucker stood between Jake and their younger brother Evan at the front of the Shelby Lake Community Church, but this time, they wore black tuxes. Tucker wore a navy vest and bow tie, while Jake's was pink.

Their youngest brother, Micah, hadn't shown, and Tucker tried not to let that disappointment get him down.

With hands clasped in front of him, Tucker scanned the gathered family and friends seated in oak pews with crimson padding to match the carpeting. As his eyes searched the rows, he spied Bella seated in the back pew. His heart smacked against his ribs. Dressed in a white button-down blouse and black pants with her hair twisted in a bun, she smiled at him and gave him a subtle wink that made him feel sixteen all over again.

As Alec Seaver played his guitar, Tori's two brides-maids—her sister, Kendra, and her boss, Sophia—glided down the aisle in navy dresses that brushed their knees. Behind them, Landon, dressed identically to Tucker, walked between Olivia and Annabeth, Tori's niece, down the aisle.

Olivia and Annabeth wore matching short-sleeved blush-pink dresses with fluffy skirts that flared when they twirled, which they'd done at every opportunity. A band of navy roses wrapped around their tiny waists. Their hair had been curled and held back with a band of flowers that matched the ones in the baskets they carried.

Landon took his role as ring bearer seriously. With his hair slicked back and chin held high, he stared straight ahead as he walked between the girls.

The girls headed for Tori's sister and her boss. The moment Landon reached Tucker, he looked up at him. "Look, Dad. I told you I could do it."

His loud voice caused a few snickers among the small

group of family and friends. Tucker held his hand out for a subtle high five.

Tucker heard Jake's quick intake of breath and looked away from his son to the bride who had stolen his brother's heart.

With Claudia's hand linked through her elbow, Tori captured Jake's eyes and held them as she walked toward him. Her blush-pink gown and long veil trailing down the back of her pinned-up hair made her look like a model from a bridal magazine.

For the next twenty minutes, Tucker tried to focus on Pastor Nate's message about second chances, but his gaze kept wandering to the back row, where Bella had been sitting.

Jake and Tori exchanged their vows, and Jake kissed his bride. Tucker and Evan whistled. Later, at the back of the church, family and friends gathered around the newlyweds, clapping and hugging the couple.

Over the tops of their heads, Tucker searched the crowd for Bella, but she must have slipped back to the barn to get ready for the reception.

Once the bride and groom accepted their congratulations from the well-wishers and assembled the wedding party and family for what seemed like half a million photos, everyone made their way through town and up the hill to the barn.

Long strands of lights zigzagged between the barn beams, casting a softened glow across the polished wooden floor and over the buffet tables covered in white tablecloths that ran down the middle of the barn. Round tables covered with navy tablecloths and pale pink runners and mismatched vases of flowers sat on both sides of the buffet tables.

Tucker herded Olivia and Landon toward the bridal

table, but the moment they saw Bella in her chef whites standing near the buffet table, they veered toward her and flung their arms around her legs.

Maneuvering them away from the hot chafing dishes, Bella knelt and wrapped them in her arms. "You guys did such a great job. I'm so proud of you. And you look so awesome, too."

"Izzie, watch me." Olivia stepped out of her arms and twirled so her skirt would flare.

"How fun. I'm so jealous of your twirly skirt. Maybe I could borrow your dress sometime?"

"Oh, Izzie. You're so silly. My dress won't fit you."

Bella stuck out her bottom lip. "It won't? Well, that's a bummer."

"She's good with them." Holding a steaming foam cup of coffee, Dad stood next to Tucker with one hand shoved in the pocket of his trousers.

"Yes, she is. And they adore her, too."

"The two of you are spending a lot of time together."

"She's worth spending time with. Besides, we're good friends."

"Seems to me there's more to it than that."

He wasn't quite sure how to answer that.

Tucker eyed his father's coffee, wishing he had his own cup. He shifted his gaze from the beautiful chef laughing with his children to the polished gleam on the toe of his shoe. "I'm thinking it's time."

"For what?"

"To move forward."

Dad drew in a breath and let it out slowly. Then he nodded and smiled. "For me, it was more than knowing it was okay to move on. It was wanting to do it. After your mother was killed, the last thing I imagined was getting remarried. I just couldn't see having a new life with someone else. Your mother and I were married nearly thirty years. We had four great boys and managed a family business together. How could I let someone else into my life after that? But she was gone. I couldn't live in the past. Thing was, though, falling in love with Claudia wasn't something I set out to do. It just happened. Give it up to God, son. He'll steer you in the right direction."

"Problem is, I'm a package deal. Not a lot of women want a ready-made family."

Dad ran a hand over his jaw and jerked his head toward the topic of their discussion. "Isabella isn't like a lot of women. I doubt she's going to have a problem with the whole package."

Dad's words rang in Tucker's head all through dinner. Even though he tried to focus on the conversation at his table, he kept watching Bella as she refilled the trays of food. Then when dinner concluded, Kathy, Dana and Noel—Joe's servers from the diner—helped her clear the buffet tables and break them down to make more room.

When the band switched from dinner music to dance music, Tucker did the obligatory dances with the bridal party, then Tori and finally Claudia. But his eyes stayed focused on Bella's movements.

When she slipped out the barn door, Tucker excused himself and hurried after her.

He stepped outside to find her sitting on one of the benches with her back to him. She had removed her chef jacket, and it lay folded next to her along with her hat. She tugged the pins from her hair and fluffed her fingers through it as soft waves floated around her shoulders. She shivered. After putting the hairpins in her front pocket, she rubbed her hands together to generate some heat.

He shrugged out of his dinner jacket and moved silently behind her to wrap it around her shoulders.

She started and whirled around, shooting him a wide-eyed look. Then she smiled.

And his heart puddled in the pit of his stomach.

He sat next to her and slid an arm around her shoulders. "You were amazing tonight. Dinner went so smoothly."

"You didn't notice my freak-out when I spilled half a pan of roasted potatoes?"

"No, and I don't think anyone else did, either. You're a natural, Bella. Have you considering becoming a full-time caterer?"

She shrugged. "I don't know. Maybe someday. Right now, there's no time for anything else. Not with helping Dad with the diner now that George walked off. Dad doesn't seem to be in a hurry to replace him until business picks up."

"I thought business was going well?"

"The first couple of weeks were crazy busy, but now that the newness has worn off, we're dying again. I don't get it. We're serving quality food. Sure, we had to raise prices a little, but come on. Dad hadn't raised prices in years. I love the idea of catering, but right now, that feels overwhelming. I'm almost too afraid to get my hopes up only to have them dashed again. Honestly, that dream just feels almost impossible."

"Nothing's impossible with God."

"Right."

"You don't sound convinced."

"I admire your faith, Tucker. I do. But I just haven't had the same experiences with God blessing me or answering prayers the way you have."

"Have you tried?"

She lifted a shoulder. "What's the point? Just when I start to trust someone, I get hurt. I've dealt with enough disappointments not to put my hopes in someone I can't even see."

"The beauty of faith is believing without seeing and knowing in your heart God will be there with you, no matter what. He loves you, Bella. More than you could ever imagine. All you have to do is take that first step."

"You make it sound so easy."

Tucker laughed. "In theory, yes, it's a piece of cake, but actually doing it is tough. It's stripping away all your protective armor and being vulnerable and exposed with your heart. And no one likes that for fear of rejection. But God doesn't hurt you. He'll never reject you."

She didn't say anything for a few minutes, then she looked at Tucker with eyes glazed with tears. "How can God love me when my own mother walked away?"

"Because He wants only one thing from you."

"What's that?"

"Your heart."

"What if…what if I can't give it to Him?"

"Then you'll miss out on incredible blessings He has in store for you. One of my favorite passages of Scripture comes from Jeremiah 29. 'For I know the thoughts that I think toward you, saith the Lord, thoughts of peace, and not of evil, to give you an expected end. Then shall ye call upon me, and ye shall go and pray unto me, and I will hearken unto you. And ye shall seek me, and find me, when ye shall search for me with all your heart.'"

"That's lovely."

"Yes, but within those words are such truth and promise—God has a plan for each one of us, a plan to prosper us, to give us a hope and a future. However, that doesn't mean our lives are going be without struggles. We grow through our struggles. Sure, we hate going through them, but when we put our trust in God,

He helps us through them and we grow closer to Him. Walking with God and growing with Him brings us the ultimate joy. Learning to trust, even when it's hard, begins with a simple prayer of asking for His help."

"How can you hold on to your faith after everything you've gone through—the tornado, losing your mom, losing Rayne—all of it?"

"I'm not gonna lie, it's been tough. But even during the hard stuff, God's there with the promise that the season will pass. We become resilient and our faith grows. He wants us to depend on Him at all times—in the good and in the bad."

"You're a good man, Tucker." Bella cupped his cheek.

"You're not so bad yourself." He looked into her eyes, seeing his own reflection, and brushed her hair off her forehead. He traced the curve of her cheekbone as his eyes dropped to her mouth. He lowered his head and captured her lips, kissing her gently.

She wove her arm around his neck and pressed her hand against the back of his head, pulling him closer. He wrapped his arms around her shoulders and drew her into his embrace.

The warmth of her touch, the whisper of her breath against his cheek and caress of her fingers along his neck unlocked feelings and emotions imprisoned by years of grief. He pressed her head against his chest, aware of his heart pounding against her cheek. "Isabella Bradley, I'm so glad you came home."

"Me, too." Her words muffled against the threads of his tuxedo shirt.

He tipped her chin. Her pink cheeks showed she'd been affected by their kiss. But the frown between her brows and the sadness that colored her eyes made him question if those feelings were one-sided.

He wasn't going to apologize for the kiss. But was he asking too much from her too soon? What if God wasn't the only one she couldn't give her heart to? What if she couldn't give it to him, either? Was he able to be okay with that? What other choice did he have?

"Getting back to the catering conversation—maybe you need a partner."

"Are you applying for the job?"

"Depends."

"On what?"

"Whether you're referring to work…or something else." Before she could reply, he brushed his lips over hers once again.

She pulled back and looked at him with questioning eyes. Her lashes fluttered closed as she pressed her forehead to his chest. "What are we doing?"

He tipped her chin up and smiled. "I was trying to kiss you."

She cupped her hand over his. "I know, but—"

"No buts." He caressed her cheekbone with his finger. His voice lowered to a hoarse whisper. "I want to kiss you again. May I?"

Her eyes searched his, then she nodded.

Cupping a hand gently around the side of her neck, he lowered his mouth to hers again.

Her hands settled on his shoulders as she shifted closer to him.

"Daddy, why are you kissing Izzie? Are you getting married like Uncle Jake? Is Izzie going to be our new mommy? Yay! I'm so 'cited!"

Tucker and Bella jerked apart. Heat tinged his ears as he faced his daughter dancing around and clapping her hands.

He scrubbed a hand over his face.

Oh brother. How was he going to handle this one?

* * *

After tossing and turning again last night, Isabella had risen even more exhausted and, if she dared voice it—a bit conflicted. Not only had she relived that kiss a million times, but she continued to replay the conversation with Tucker about trusting God, and then his suggestion about partnering with her catering business, which still felt out of reach, especially with the diner's current situation.

She'd pulled her neglected Bible out of her nightstand drawer and read the passage in Jeremiah that Tucker had referenced last night. She still didn't get how someone could learn how to thrive while going through struggles. It just didn't make sense.

Isabella couldn't get Tucker's words out of her head… or the memory of his kiss out of her heart.

Oh boy.

She was setting herself up for trouble.

With many of her friends already married and having kids, she seemed behind, but was that really what she wanted?

For years, she had wanted to establish her career, preferably in her own kitchen.

But now that she'd been back home in Shelby Lake, the only one she'd even consider a future with was Tucker.

The way he kissed her suggested he was ready to let someone into his life, and after their conversation yesterday, it seemed like the next move was up to her.

The memory of his kiss burrowed deep in her heart—the softness of his lips, the scent of his cologne, the gentleness of his touch.

She sighed.

She hadn't felt that way in such a long time.

Or maybe even ever.

But now wasn't the time to think about that.

She had other pressing needs that demanded her attention, like figuring out how to keep the diner open.

As she'd mentioned to Tucker, the reopening had been a success, generating a greater-than-expected surge in sales, but then business had dropped off more than she'd expected.

Kathy, Dana and Noel had mentioned a few of Dad's regulars grumbling about the increased prices, the new menu and the food not tasting the same. Maybe because it wasn't covered in a layer of grease.

She gave the prep station a final rinse and dried her hands.

In the dining room, Noel and Dana refilled condiments and returned them to the tables. They used ketchup bottles as microphones and sang along to a new pop song playing from one of their phones.

Bells over the door jangled against the glass, and the music stopped abruptly.

Isabella peered over the pass bar, but she couldn't see who had entered the diner. The girls talked with the whomever it was, and Isabella returned to finishing up in the kitchen.

Noel pushed open the swinging kitchen door. "Hey, Bella, there's some guy here to see you."

"Tucker?"

"No. I haven't seen this guy before, but I sure wish I had. Yummy." She waggled her eyebrows.

Isabella rolled her eyes. "I'll be out in a second."

She washed and dried her hands, then shut off the lights before heading to the dining room. She rounded the corner and stopped suddenly, her mouth dry as dust.

"Justin. What are you doing here?"

Justin Wilkes stood near the breakfast counter wearing fashionable skinny jeans, an untucked button-down shirt and a dark brown V-necked pullover sweater. His hundred-dollar haircut had been stylishly tousled.

A couple of months ago, if he had walked into the diner, she would've had to force herself not to beg for her old job back.

Tonight, though, his unexpected presence felt more like…annoyance.

"Isabella, look at you." He took her hands and held her at a distance.

She glanced down at her dirty apron and shook her head. Of course he'd have to wait until she'd finished cleaning to walk into the place.

"What are you doing here?" She rested an elbow on the counter and made no move to offer him a seat.

He shot her a boyish grin that worked on so many other women. But she was immune to his charm. "I made a mistake, Isabella, in firing you. I've come to say I'm sorry. I left the Briarwood, and I'm opening my own restaurant. I want you to be my head chef."

The words she'd dreamed of hearing for years bounced around in her head. "Wait. What? When did you leave? And why me?"

"I left about a month ago. The kitchen was falling apart without your organization. I decided I wanted to open my own place and have total control—it's a small bistro. Nothing fancy yet, but once you come on board, you can create those dishes that people raved about at the Briarwood."

"Justin, I was a saucier. I'm not a head chef. I don't have the experience."

"You will gain it at my place. Come on, Isabella. Say yes."

"You fired me. And after you learned the truth about

what happened, not once did you call and apologize. Or even offer me my job back."

"I was a jerk. I admit it. But now you can leave this dive behind." He waved a dismissive hand over the diner. "And work in a real kitchen."

"Hey, this is a real kitchen. My dad's owned this place for twenty-five years, and he can cook circles around you any day of the week."

He scoffed and rolled his eyes. "You're always going to be a greasy spoon girl, aren't you?" He pulled a business card out of his shirt pocket. "Here's my card. Think about it and let me know if you'd like to take your career places. You have a week, then I'll need an answer."

Isabella took his card and didn't say anything as he turned on his heel and headed out the door.

Her own kitchen. And all she had to do was say yes. But could she handle Justin's arrogance?

And what about her dad's diner? And Tucker?

Suddenly having her own kitchen didn't seem as appealing as it once had.

Chapter Twelve

When Brandon and Harrison, two of his fellow paramedics, suggested lunch after their training, Tucker enticed them to consider the diner by recommending an order of Joe's garbage fries. Truth was, he couldn't care less about the food—he wanted to see Bella.

Since Jake and Tori's wedding, he hadn't seen her as much as he'd like, especially now that Willow was caring for Olivia and Landon. He kept coming up with excuses to swing by the diner on the off chance he'd see her, but she'd been too busy in the kitchen to give him much attention.

They needed time with just the two of them to sort out where their relationship was going.

He loved being her friend, but if that was all they were destined to be, then he needed to stop kissing her.

Which was going to be a challenge.

He pulled the glass door open and stepped back, allowing his buddies to pass before joining them to search for a booth. The diner was full, but a couple left a booth that would give him great visibility into the kitchen through the pass-through window.

As he walked past the breakfast counter, he looked

over the open area into the kitchen, where Bella, dressed in her chef whites, stood head down focusing on the flat top and six-burner.

He collided with someone and swung his attention back to the dining room.

Joe.

Perfect.

The tips of his ears caught fire as his buddies' laughter echoed through the diner. "Sorry, Joe." Heat scalded his face. "I wasn't watching where I was going."

The man scowled at him. "Pay less attention to my daughter and more attention to where you're going and you wouldn't be knocking into people and spilling their coffee."

"Yes, sir." He started to pass, then he turned back to Bella's father. "Hey, Joe, have you given any more thought to the community garden project?"

"I told you once, I'm not the man you want."

"Actually, you are—"

"Holland, I've never thrown anyone out of my place, but if you don't stop badgering me about this, there will be a first time for everything." Without another word, he pushed past Tucker and barreled into the kitchen.

Tucker slid into the booth across from Brandon and Harrison and stared at the menu. The growl in Joe's voice rolled around in his head. The man's demeanor had changed in the last few months. There had to been more than blood sugar issues at play.

Noel, their server, appeared with a coffeepot. "Morning, boys. Coffee?"

The three of them slid their white stoneware mugs toward her. After filling their cups, she set the steaming pot on the table and pulled an ordering pad out of her black apron pocket.

"Today's lunch special is the Liberty burger with baked sweet potato fries and maple mustard, broiled flounder with lemon pepper, steamed broccoli on a bed of brown rice, and garden vegetable soup made from locally sourced produce and served with a side salad and multigrain roll."

Brandon and Harrison looked at each other, then flipped the placemat menu over.

Harrison scowled and swiveled in his seat to look around the diner. "Are we at Joe's? What's with all the fancy dishes? What happened to Joe's prize-winning chili or the deluxe cheeseburger and garbage fries?"

Noel smiled at them. "They're still on the menu. I was just telling you today's specials."

"Oh good. For a minute, I thought Isabella had changed more than the decor."

"Knock it off. A salad wouldn't hurt any of us. Besides, your arteries will thank you."

Harrison burst out laughing and elbowed his buddy.

Noel kept her smile in place, but she seemed to be losing patience. "Hey, guys, pick on each other later. I have other tables to tend to while I've got them."

Tucker frowned. "What's that mean?"

"The first couple of weeks, the diner was packed, but then people started complaining about the food not tasting the same. They want the greasy burgers and onion rings, not salads and baked fish."

"Bella's just trying to offer healthier options. Joe's burgers are still on the menu."

"It's not the same. But after her meeting with some restaurant owner who came in to talk with her yesterday, we all think her days in Shelby Lake are numbered."

"Why do you say that?"

Noel eyed the counter, then leaned in and lowered her

voice. "I'm not one to gossip, and I'm only telling you because you helped her fix this place up. But that city dude offered her a head chef position in a new restaurant he was opening."

"Is she taking it?"

"I heard her say she'd think about it. He gave her a week to get back to him."

"Does Joe know?"

Noel shrugged. "Not sure. You wanna know more, you'll have to talk to her or Joe. You guys know what you want or should I come back? "

Tucker cupped his coffee mug. "I'll have a cheeseburger and Joe's garbage fries."

Brandon nodded to Noel. "Make that two."

"Make that three."

Noel smiled. "Easy enough."

She left and Tucker took a sip of his coffee, then grimaced and reached for the creamer. As he stirred in the milk, Noel's words tumbled inside his head. Was Bella truly thinking about leaving? Running her own kitchen had been her dream, but why hadn't she said anything to him about the offer? Maybe he'd misread their relationship, but he'd felt like they were moving toward something. But maybe she wanted to remain friends for this very reason.

His phone rang, and he pulled it out of his pocket to see Willow's face on the screen. "Hey, Willow. What's up?"

"I was wondering if Livie and Landon could spend the night at my house tonight? Mom and Dad are in town for my birthday and want to see them."

"Sure, of course. How long are they visiting?"

"Just for the weekend."

"Let me know when you'd like me to drop them off."

Willow hesitated a moment. "How about if I pick them up?"

"Craig and Shari still blame me for not being able to save Rayne." It wasn't a question but a statement of fact. "Don't worry about it, Will. You can pick them up from school. I've added you as an emergency contact, but I'll still send in a note to their teachers."

"Thanks, Tucker. I'm sorry it has to be this way. My parents are still grieving and want to blame someone for their loss, even if it's misplaced."

"Don't worry about it."

He ended the call. His appetite gone, he pulled out his wallet and threw two twenties on the table. "Hey, guys, lunch is on me. Ask Noel to box up my burger and fries. Drop it off at the station, if you would. I need to take care of something."

He pushed through the door and headed outside, the crisp air cooling his face.

"Tucker."

He turned to find Bella standing outside the rear kitchen door in her white chef jacket and pinstriped black pants, her hair pulled back and tucked under her chef hat. She looked completely out of place.

She did not belong in Shelby Lake with her chef whites, gourmet menu and big dreams.

"Hey, Bella. How's it going?" He stuffed his hands in his front pockets to keep from pulling her into his arms.

"Busy. No wonder Dad's always bushed after the diner closes every day."

"How's he doing? I ran into him earlier…like literally."

She giggled, the sound shooting through him. "Yeah, he mentioned you'd spilled his coffee before he stomped upstairs to change."

Tucker shook his head. "I was a little distracted."

"He mentioned that, too." She gave him a soft smile.

"Willow's parents are in town to celebrate her birthday and they want to see Livie and Landon, so Willow's going to pick them up after school and keep them overnight. I wondered if you would like to come for dinner tonight—just the two of us. I'll cook for you."

"I've never had someone cook for me like that. I would love to come to dinner tonight. Thank you for asking."

"Great, it's a date." He reached for her fingers and gave them a gentle squeeze.

Tonight, he planned to let her know how he felt and see where their relationship was headed. He didn't want to stand in the way of her dreams, but he couldn't stay quiet any longer about how he felt about her.

Isabella couldn't stop smiling.

For the next hour, she finished the tickets on the wheel, focusing on flipping burgers, making salads and breaking eggs a little harder than necessary.

Once Kathy locked the door behind the last customer, Isabella poured herself the remaining cup of coffee in the pot, stirred in cream and sugar, put on some music in the kitchen, and began prepping for tomorrow.

She reached for the clipboard holding the prep list. It slipped out of her hands and fell against her cup, spilling coffee across the paper, the food service counter and onto the floor.

Isabella snatched a kitchen towel and pressed it against the clipboard, then cleaned up the spilled coffee.

The door to Dad's office opened, and a man in a navy suit and red patterned tie and carrying a briefcase stepped out. His short dark hair had been slicked back, and he removed dark-framed glasses and deposited them in his inside suit pocket before shaking her father's hand.

"Thanks for your time, Joe. I look forward to hearing from you."

"I'll be in touch."

But even though Dad gave the man a firm handshake and had a smile in place, sadness shadowed his eyes and bracketed his mouth.

Instead of going through the kitchen and walking out the front door, the man left through the rear kitchen door.

"Dad, who was that?"

Dad scrubbed a hand over his face. "Bella, we need to talk." He turned and headed back into his office, leaving the door open.

Her stomach turned over as she forced herself to head into his office and face whatever grim news he had to share.

She pressed a shoulder against the doorjamb. "What's going on?"

"That man was Leonard Terroni, and he made me an offer on the diner."

"Offer? What sort of offer?"

"An offer to buy it. At a good price."

"Why?"

"What do you mean, why?"

"Why would he offer to buy when the diner's not even for sale?"

"Listen, Bella—"

"No, you listen, Dad. I came home several weeks ago and found you passed out on the floor with a fire starting in the kitchen. Then I spent a week painting and updating the diner and advertising on social media, and then several more weeks running the kitchen nearly single-handedly to save your dream, only to have you consider selling the place without even talking to me first?" Tears burned her eyes.

"But no one asked you to. You charged in here making changes and refused to listen to my objections."

She waved a hand over the restaurant. "You're saying I did this against your will?"

Dad leaned forward, elbows on his desk, and cradled his head in his hands. Then he leaned back and rested his head on the back of his chair. "I'm not blaming this on you. I could've stopped you, but I was just too tired. I've been tired for a very long time."

"Then let's call your doctor and get some lab work done to make sure your sugar levels are where they need to be."

"My blood sugar's fine. This has nothing to do with my health. I appreciate everything you've done to help save the diner, Bella, but I just want to sell the place and retire. Leonard's offer is a good one—I can pay off the bank loan, repay you and then decide where I want to settle."

"Settle? You're thinking of leaving Shelby Lake? And all of this work to try and save the diner was for nothing? And what about me, Dad? Where do I fit in your plans?"

"You can return to New York where you belong and build your career."

"I don't have a career. I was fired, remember? I have nothing to return to."

"Isabella, you're young, with your whole life ahead of you. You can go anywhere and build your career."

"But I came home to help you."

"No, you came home to hide. This is your safety net, as home should be, but I didn't pay for four years of culinary school for you to waste your talents here. Now's the time to dust yourself off and face your future."

Future? What future?

Everything she wanted was crumbling around her, and she had no say and no way to stop it.

Isabella left her father's office and returned to the kitchen. Until the sale of the diner was finalized, she still needed to be ready for the next day. And that meant prepping for a couple of hours. Maybe the tedious work would take her mind of the feelings of abandonment rattling around in her heart.

As she cut up potatoes for tomorrow's home fries, her phone rang. She removed her gloves and picked it up.

Justin's name and number appeared on the screen.

She sighed, set down her knife and answered the phone. "Hello?"

"Isabella, I'm calling for your answer."

"Yesterday you said I had a week." Isabella's eyes darted toward Dad's open office door. His seat was empty, but she hadn't heard him leave. He was probably calling Leonard to finalize the sale. She pressed her back against the counter and rubbed a thumb and forefinger over her gritty eyes.

"Isabella, are you there?"

"I'm here, Justin. I'm thinking."

"I figured you would have had plenty of time to think by now."

"Yes, but there have been some new developments for me to consider."

"What? Another offer? What is it? I'll offer you more."

"Why do you even want me working for you, Justin?"

"Because you're good. You're levelheaded and work well under pressure. And your food is amazing."

"Will I have a say in how the kitchen is run?"

"Well, I'll consider your input, of course."

"You know, Justin, I've wanted to run my own kitchen

from the moment I enrolled in culinary school. Working at the Briarwood gave me an opportunity to hone my skills and learn new experiences. But when you fired me, I was crushed."

"You know why I had to, right?"

"No, actually, I don't. You didn't believe in me, and when you learned the truth, you didn't have the backbone to stand up to management to have me reinstated."

"Come on, Isabella. Let's put that behind us and start fresh. I'm offering you a great opportunity here."

"A great opportunity, sure. Until something doesn't go your way or you bow to pressure. Then what? You're going to fire me again? I don't want that kind of risk. You've shown me what kind of man you are, and that's not someone I want to work with. Even though I'm uncertain about my future right now, I've decided to stay where I am and see where God leads me."

"Whatever. You won't get another opportunity like this again, and don't bother asking me to write you a reference, because that's not going to happen. Enjoy your small-town life, Isabella. It seems I was right—you'll never be more than a greasy spoon girl after all."

The line went silent.

Isabella gripped her phone so tightly her knuckles ached.

She pulled on a fresh pair of gloves and picked up her knife. Tears filled her eyes, and she tried to blink them back so she could see where she was cutting. After nearly nicking her finger with the tip of the blade, Isabella dropped the knife on the counter.

An ache that uncoiled from the pit of her stomach snaked up through her chest, threatening to split apart her ribs and shatter her heart into a million pieces.

If she had half a brain in her head, she would have

jumped at Justin's offer. But he'd shown his real colors when he fired her, and she didn't want to work for him again.

Now Dad was trying to push her out of the nest, but how could she fly with broken wings?

Despite her hard work and desire to partner with him, it wasn't enough.

She wasn't enough.

And she didn't know what to do about that.

Or where to go from here.

Perhaps tonight Tucker could offer her some insight and help her to figure out what to do, because for the first time since returning to Shelby Lake, she felt completely lost.

Chapter Thirteen

Tonight was most definitely a date.

Unlike her uncertainty about attending the farmers market as friends a few weeks ago, Tucker had made it clear tonight was going to be just the two of them.

To talk.

For someone who loved to cook, having someone else doing the cooking ranked up there with one of her all-time favorite romantic ideas.

She had curled her hair, then pulled it over to one side to fall in front of her shoulder. She added another pin and did a final twirl in front of the mirror to make sure the back of her emerald-green dress was wrinkle-free. A quick spritz of her favorite but seldom used perfume, and she reached for her phone just as it rang.

Her friend Jeanne's face appeared on the screen.

"Hey, Jeanne. What's going on?" She slipped her feet into a pair of nude strappy sandals. Her toes would probably freeze, but she didn't care. Tonight would be worth it. She grabbed her purse on her way out the door.

"Bella, I just talked to Justin. He mentioned you turned down his offer to be head chef at his new restaurant."

"Why would I want to work for him again after he fired me?"

"Would you consider returning to the Briarwood, at least for a short period of time?"

"Why? What's going on?"

"Your mother's going to be here." Jeanne spoke so quietly that Isabella must've misunderstood.

"What? My what?"

"I didn't mean for it to come out like that."

Isabella sat on the edge of her bed and gripped her phone. "How about you tell me what's going on?"

For the next ten minutes, she listened to her friend's explanation and then hung up with scrambled thoughts tossing inside her head. With her heart racing and body trembling, Isabella headed for her car.

Somehow, she made it up the hill. Somehow, she managed to park in his driveway. And somehow, she needed to get out of her car, go inside and tell Tucker she needed to cancel their date.

Gripping the top of the steering wheel, she blew out a breath and pressed her forehead against her hands.

Why did Jeanne have to call now? Why couldn't she have called after Isabella's dinner with Tucker?

The cold bit her cheeks and the smell of snow swirled through the air as she stepped out of the car, which hadn't had time to heat up during the short drive up the hill. In her daze over Jeanne's call, she realized she'd left without a coat, the air blowing through her and stroking her bones.

Shivering, she hurried up the walk to the front door, but before she could knock, the door opened.

Tucker stood in the halo of the front porch light wearing dark gray dress pants and a royal-blue dress shirt open at the throat.

Her heart slipped in her chest.

He gave her a slow, easy smile. "Hey. I'm glad you could come. Hope you're hungry."

She played with the strap of her purse. "Listen, Tucker, I can't stay."

His eyebrows puckered. "Can't stay? Why not?"

She shivered. "The thing is, I need to leave."

"At least come in out of the cold and tell me what's going on."

She stepped inside, the warmth of his home enveloping her.

Her gave her a half smile and wrapped one of her curls around his finger. "You look gorgeous. And that dress... man, Bella. You know how to ruin a guy's concentration."

His words warmed her from the inside out. "Thank you."

The dining room table had been dressed with a cream-colored cloth, glistening stemware and white china with tiny blue flowers. A low bouquet of her favorite peach-colored roses sat between two chunky, lit vanilla candles sitting on turned wooden bases. The rich scent of roasted meat filled the air.

The perfect evening with the perfect guy.

And she was going to ruin it.

"Everything looks amazing, Tucker."

"Stay and eat with me. I made garlic butter steaks, roasted potatoes with rosemary and olive oil, pastry-wrapped asparagus, and molten lava cake for dessert."

"I'm impressed. Maybe you're the one who should be opening a restaurant."

"Say the word, and I'll be your partner."

If only...

He shoved his hands in his front pockets. "So why can't you stay?"

"I need to leave tonight."

"Where are you going?"

"Back to the Briarwood."

"They hired you back?"

"Not quite. My friend Jeanne called as I was getting ready to leave for your place to say she's catering an event and thinks I should be a part of it."

"What sort of event?"

"A book signing and a competition of sorts—all promotional activities for Solange Boucher's current book tour."

"Your mother is in the country?"

Isabella clasped her hands, dropped her gaze to her fingers and nodded slowly. "Apparently there's a cooking competition going on, and the winner will win fifty thousand dollars and be given the opportunity to intern with Solange and be a part of her cooking show staff."

"And you want to be a part of that?"

"I know it sounds a bit delusional, but if I enter this competition, then I can help Dad pay off his loan, and I can show my mother I have what it takes to be the right kind of daughter for her."

Tucker reached for Isabella's hands. "Bella, I know how much you want to be a part of your mother's life, but do you think this is the best way to do this?"

"I don't know. Probably not. But I need to see her."

"And if you win? Then what? You go to France and leave everything behind? What about Joe? The diner? Your dream of running your own kitchen? What about your new job offer?"

"Dad's selling the diner. And how do you know about the job offer?"

"What do you mean, your dad's selling the diner? Since when?"

"Since this afternoon. He met with Leonard Terroni, who offered him a good price on the diner. He wants to sell and retire. It's been quite a day."

"Apparently." He took a step closer. "And where does this leave us?"

Her breathed hitched. "Us?"

"You and me." Tucker brushed her hair away from her face. "If you leave Shelby Lake, where does that leave us?"

Isabella covered his hand with hers and gently pulled it away. "I don't know."

A shadow passed over Tucker's face as he took a step back. "I see."

"Tucker…"

"No, Bella, I get it. Your career needs to come first, right? You've worked hard for this. I can't thank you enough for everything you've done for my family. I love the way you've bonded with my children, giving me peace about leaving them in your hands. I truly appreciate everything you've done, and I value your friendship more than you'll ever know. I wish you well on your future pursuits."

He valued her friendship?

So maybe she had misread tonight and it wasn't a date after all.

She lifted her eyes to him, then frowned. "You're talking like this is…goodbye."

"Isn't it?"

"I don't know. Maybe it's one huge mistake that's going to blow up in my face. I should just call Jeanne back and tell her I can't come."

"And you'll regret it—and maybe even me—if you don't try. You've worked so hard to get where you are, and you don't want to miss out on these opportunities to see where they can take you."

"And just where am I? I'm an unemployed chef standing in for others and butting heads with my father, who doesn't seem to want me here. Maybe you're right. Maybe it's time to stop being the stand-in and go for the starring role. Goodbye, Tucker." She reached up and touched his cheek, then brushed a final kiss across his lips.

Without another word, she rushed out the door and hurried to her car as the broken look on his face wrapped around her heart and squeezed the breath from her lungs.

What had she done?

When Tucker mapped out the evening in his head, nowhere had he expected Bella to walk away without even staying for dinner. But it was probably better to have her leave now than after his children had become more emotionally invested.

Or him.

Tucker gripped the back of the dining room chair and stared at the table set for two.

Did he really think using his grandmother's china and lighting candles he'd picked up at the grocery store would be enough to convince Bella he wanted to be more than friends?

Guess Joe was right after all—she'd only come home to lick her wounds. She wasn't meant for small-town life.

Or with a rescuer who came as a package deal.

Tucker blew out the candles. He opened the door to the china closet built in under the stairs and pulled out the protective cases for his grandmother's dishes. After putting the dinnerware away, he carried the water goblets to the sink and poured out the liquid. As he moved to turn them upside down on the drying mat, one of the stems knocked against the faucet.

The goblet flew out of his hand and crashed against the stainless-steel sink.

He stared at the countless broken pieces that seemed like a perfect metaphor for his love life. Gripping the sink, a shudder welled up between his ribs, creating a burning so fierce it made his face twist.

His breath came out in short bursts as he struggled to keep from crying like a baby in front of his kitchen sink.

Heaving a sigh, Tucker picked out the larger pieces and tossed them in the trash can under the sink. As he reached for a smaller shard, it sliced the pad of his thumb, dripping blood over the remaining pieces.

For a moment, he wanted to scream and shout about the battle raging between his head and his heart.

He should have known better than to cross the line of friendship. Asking for anything more was setting himself up for a continual dull ache in his chest that never quite healed.

He had his family. He had his kids. Couldn't that be enough?

No.

Not anymore.

He wanted the whole package. He'd had it once and thought it was gone again forever, but Bella coming back into his life showed his heart was ready for more.

Then she'd walked out the door, abandoning what they could have together and leaving him feeling broken and scattered.

He cleaned up the rest of the mess and then wrapped a Band-Aid around his thumb.

What was he going to do about the food? He grabbed

his phone off the counter and tapped out a text to his dad. Eat yet?

Nah. Watching a game. Will grab something in a bit.

Bringing down dinner.

What about your date?

Will explain in 5.

Tucker grabbed some storage containers out of the cabinet and filled them with the steak, potatoes and asparagus. He added cake to the other one. After changing out of his dress clothes into a pair of sweats, he put on his jacket, grabbed the food and headed outside.

The evening chill crept down his neck. The crunch of his steps through the dried leaves broke the stillness of the darkness as he trekked down the road to the farmhouse, where the front porch light shined brightly, beckoning him to find solace for his pain.

He was fine.

Or at least he would be.

He'd survived greater pain than this.

He just had to keep moving. One foot in front of the other.

He entered the farmhouse without knocking and headed to the kitchen as sounds of the game filtered from the family room.

Tucker opened the cabinet and pulled out two plates, filled them, then tossed one in the microwave.

Bella didn't need to know he'd watched YouTube videos to see how to make the pastry-wrapped asparagus. And she didn't need to know he'd pored through his mother's old cookbooks searching for her recipe for molten lava cake.

Wasted effort to impress a girl who didn't want to be a part of his life.

Grabbing steak knives, forks and napkins, he carried the food into the family room. Dad lay stretched out on the couch, but when he saw Tucker, he jumped to his feet and reached for one of the plates.

He inhaled. "Smells good. What is it?"

Tucker listed the food he'd made for Bella.

"What happened to dinner?"

"She got a better offer." Tucker sat on the matching leather chair and cut off a bite of steak. Then he set the plate on the coffee table, his appetite gone, and rested his elbows on his knees. Cupping both sides of his head, he told Dad about his conversation with Bella.

"I thought we'd be enough for her, but I guess I was wrong."

"Son, this isn't about you or anything you're lacking. It's about Isabella wanting something she hasn't had for years—a relationship with her mother. And honestly, you can't blame her for that."

"I know, and it would be selfish to stand in the way of that, but she seemed to think it was an either-or thing, and she wouldn't be able to have both."

"So instead of standing in her way, you stood aside."

"She kind of blindsided me with her news. And it didn't seem to be the right time to tell her how I felt."

"So you let her walk away. You risked your heart and ended up getting hurt."

"Something like that. I should've realized I had my happily-ever-after already."

"Tucker, you're no stranger to heartache, but I think that's a lie the enemy plants in your head to keep you from going after what God's mapped out for your life. Perhaps a form of self-preservation against more hurt. The Bible tells us perfect love casts out fear. And God doesn't give us a spirit of fear but one of courage and boldness."

Dad's soothing tone laced with compassion and words of wisdom chipped away at the foundation of the wall Tucker was rebuilding around his heart—the wall Bella had helped tear down each moment he spent with her.

"I know that in my head, Dad. I do. I'd planned to tell Bella how I felt, to see what a future together could be like, but I didn't get the chance. And now I have to figure out how to get over her." He drew in a ragged breath through his aching lungs. "I can't lose her, Dad. I can't go through that again."

"You love her."

Tucker paused and pressed his forehead against the palm of his hand. He swallowed several times as he realized Dad hadn't asked a question but made a statement.

"Yes." The whispered admission gave him renewed strength. He pushed away from the wall, squared his shoulders and wiped his eyes with his sleeve. "Yes, I do."

Standing, Tucker moved in front of the window, his shoulders slumped and his chin to his chest. Snow was beginning to fall, covering the grass flake by flake.

"If you love her, then make sure she knows that. And no matter what happens, God's got this…and you."

The weariness from the past few days weighed on him. He knew his father's words to be true. All he needed to do was lean into them and release his burdens.

God, I'm tired. So tired. I can't keep going like this. What do I do now?

Chapter Fourteen

Isabella had spent years not being that girl—the one who fell apart when the cute boy didn't call her—and she wasn't going to start now.

Because if she spent even half a second thinking about her ruined dinner date with Tucker, then she was going to crumble into a million pieces.

And she was not going to be that person who let someone break her heart.

Focus.

If she didn't get her head in the game and stop second-guessing herself, then she'd miss out before she had time to get her plates in front of the judges.

She'd done too much of that on the drive to the Briarwood, replaying her conversations with Tucker and her father in her head.

Was she a fool for leaving everyone she loved behind?

Especially Tucker.

Stop thinking about him.

"Jeanne, can you remove the asparagus from the oven?"

"Five more seconds." Her friend, with her blond tangle of curls pinned in a French twist and dressed in matching chef whites, gave her a thumbs-up as she reached for a pot holder and removed the pan from the oven.

Crispy-looking heads of asparagus crowned the golden pastry wrapped around it.

Isabella added oil to her cast-iron skillet and seared both sides of the rib-eye steak she'd baked in the oven on low heat. The reverse sear method will maximize flavor and moisture. Then she tossed in a couple of tablespoons of butter, let it melt and added garlic cloves and sprigs of thyme. She spooned the butter sauce over the meat, then pulled it out to rest on the cutting board while she plated the asparagus and herb-roasted potatoes.

When Jeanne managed to get her entered into the competition at the last minute, Isabella had scrambled to come up with a menu. With Tucker at the forefront of her thoughts, she'd borrowed the menu he'd prepared for their dinner.

A quick glance at the clock showed they had less than two minutes to have their plates ready for the judges.

She grabbed her chef's knife and cut through the steak, pleased to see the pink in the middle with nicely browned outer edges.

Five minutes later, Isabella stood behind the table with her hands clasped in front of her as her heart slammed against her rib cage so hard she was afraid everyone in the room could hear the beating.

In the past six years, she'd done so many events in this ballroom when she worked in the Briarwood kitchen, but she'd never been a participant.

The Briarwood ballroom, with its ivory walls, spoke of birthdays, anniversaries and wedding celebrations. Crystal chandlers hanging from the ornately tiled ceiling scattered diamonds of light across the linen-covered round tables adored with bowls of fresh flowers and filled with guests watching the competition. In the middle of the room, on the parquet dance floor, a long table covered in banquet cloths and surrounded by three chairs waited for the judges. The side door to the ballroom opened.

Chef Solange Boucher, tall and thin, dressed in a black pantsuit, led the way to the judges' table. Her dark hair with the signature silver streak was confined in a chignon at her neck. Her eyes cool and face composed, as she sat and perused the crowd. Their eyes clashed, and Isabella's breath hitched. Her mother's eyes narrowed, but then Chef Scott, the executive chef at the Briarwood, sat next to her and pulled her attention away from Isabella.

Isabella let out a sigh. When she was busy cooking, she hadn't taken the time to think about what was to come.

Justin Wilkes, Isabella's former boss, sat on the other side of Chef Scott.

Perfect.

Jeanne had said Solange Boucher was going to be the primary judge, but she wasn't sure who the other two were going to be.

Walking back into the Briarwood had been Isabella's first mistake. Entering this contest had been her second. But she couldn't back out now.

There was too much at stake.

The emcee of tonight's event walked to the center of the ballroom, and a hush fell over the room.

"Welcome to the Solange Boucher Culinary Competition."

Isabella tuned out his words at the mention of her mother's name.

"We've narrowed our finalists down to three. Our first finalist's entrée consists of seared steak with a garlic butter sauce, herb-roasted baby red potatoes and pastry-wrapped asparagus."

Servers dressed in black pants and white tuxedo shirts carried her plates to the judges. They picked up their forks and knives and cut into her steak. For a moment, the room waited in silence.

Her mother set her fork on her plate. "The steak has a nice sear and a wonderful flavor combination with the herbs and butter, but the interior of the meat is a little cool for my taste."

Justin smirked at her then nodded at her mother. "I agree. The entrée, while good, just seems a bit ordinary. I expected more from the chefs in this competition."

Chef Scott looked between the other two judges. "Sometimes simple is best. Comfort food is soothing to the soul, and this entrée speaks comfort to me, yet it showcases the chef's culinary knowledge, taking a simple meal into something that tantalizes the taste buds."

Isabella pasted a smile in place and forced her face to stay neutral. She swallowed past the clog in her throat and tuned out the rest of the comments about the other finalists' plates.

Less than an hour later, with her third-place ribbon crumpled in her pocket, Isabella headed back to her station in the kitchen to ensure it was as clean as when she found it. She washed her knives, then stowed them in her case and zipped it closed. She just wanted to leave as quickly as possible.

The memory of her humiliating career ending had resurfaced the moment she pulled onto the grounds. And now the memory would be coupled with her mother's remarks about her cooking.

The quicker she left, the quicker she could put this debacle behind her.

Isabella left the kitchen and peeked in the ballroom to see if Jeanne was still cleaning up. Finding the room empty, she turned and promptly bumped into someone.

"Oh, excuse me—" She looked up, and the rest of her words died on her lips.

"Pardonnez moi, s'il vous plaît." Her mother reached out and pressed a hand on Isabella's arm.

She looked at her mother's hand with manicured nails and opened her mouth, but she couldn't make a sound.

Her mother took a step back and started to turn.

"Wait."

Her mother turned, her cool smile in place without any recognition in her eyes. *"Oui?"*

"M-my name is Isabella Bradley. I'm your daughter."

Her mother's hand flew to her mouth as color drained from her face. *"Mais non."*

"Yes. Joe Bradley is my father. Remember him? Us?"

Her mother looked around and lowered her voice. "What are you doing here?"

"I wanted to see you. I wanted to ask why you left me twenty-five years ago crying at the airport with Dad and never came back. I've worked so hard to become a chef you could be proud of, to be the daughter you'd want back in your life." Her voice choked as tears filled her eyes. She tried holding it together. A betraying tear trailed down her cheek.

Her mother reached out a hand toward Isabella's face, but before she could touch her daughter's skin, she lowered her hand and stepped back, shaking her head. "I can't do this. I'm sorry." Her mother hurried past her and fast-walked down the hall.

Isabella stared after her, her feet frozen no matter how many times her brain screamed to go after her.

What had she expected? For her mother to take her in her arms and beg for Isabella to forgive her?

Isabella just wanted to leave. Leave the Briarwood and never set foot on the property again. It would be forever tainted by the memory of her mother walking away from her for the second time in her life.

With an ache hollowing out her chest, Isabella hurried outside to the back lot, where she'd parked her car.

This morning's snow had turned into a whiteout. She stood in the doorway of the exit trying to remember where she'd parked her car. Finding it in the second row, she stepped outside.

"Isabella."

She turned to find Dad standing outside under the awning holding a single peach rose tied with a white ribbon.

"Dad, what are you doing here?"

"I came to watch you compete."

"You were here the whole time? Why?"

"You're my daughter, and this competition was important to you. I knew what was at stake. And I didn't want you to face it alone."

"Oh Dad." She flew into his outstretched arms. He wrapped her in his embrace, holding her as the emotions she'd pushed back broke through the dam in her chest. "She didn't want me."

"I'm so sorry, sweetheart."

"I just want to go home. Back to Shelby Lake."

Dad guided her through the snow, took her keys from her hand and unlocked the doors. He settled her in the passenger seat, then rounded the car to the driver's side.

"Where's your truck? How did you get up here?"

"Tucker drove me."

"Tucker was here?"

Dad nodded. "He offered to drive me back home, but I felt like you needed me."

She pressed her head against the back of the seat. "I was an idiot for expecting more. If she wanted to see me, she would have done it way before this."

Dad gripped her hand and gave it a gentle squeeze. "I know this hurts, and you need time to process it, but you can't force others to love you. I will always be here for you."

"I love you."

"I love you, too. Let's go home."

Home.

Back to Shelby Lake. Back to the diner…for as long as they had it. Back to her ordinary life and where her heart, given time, could find wholeness again.

But could she do that without Tucker?

Maybe he was being a coward, but if Tucker could stay away from Joe's diner, then maybe he'd have a chance to get over Bella.

Since watching her competition and seeing her awarded third place—and knowing what that meant for her—he'd longed to reach out to her, but during the long drive home in blinding snow, he'd talked himself out of it.

After getting in late, he tossed and turned most of the night, and now he was dragging when he needed to pull it together to catch up on patient care reports.

Hopefully the rest of his shift would stay nice and quiet.

"Hey, Holland. You got a minute?"

Tucker jerked up to see his operations supervisor, William Franco, standing next to his desk. "Yes, sir. What's up?"

"How about coming into my office?"

He pushed away from his desk, passing the window as he headed for Franco's office. Howling winds swirled snow, creating a gray haze and limiting visibility. He found his boss standing in front of his window, his back to his open door.

His muscles tight, Tucker rapped his knuckles on the door.

Franco turned and waved him into the room as he returned to his desk. "Come in and shut the door. Have a seat."

Tucker perched on the edge of the padded chair, his gut knotted as his eyes veered to the storm outside the window. He rubbed a hand over his eyes and blew out a quiet breath. "What's up, sir?"

Franco leaned his elbows on his desk and rubbed his hands together. "I've been watching you, Tuck. You've had a tough few years, and like I said a couple of months ago, I felt like you've been burning the candle at both ends."

"I remember our previous conversation, sir, and I've put plans in place to ensure I'm giving my all on the job without distractions."

"I'm not worried about your job performance. You're the best paramedic I've seen in years. You stay focused and steady on the street, respectful of your crew, and your bravery and professionalism have been noted by those who have been watching you for the past few months. Which is why—" He paused to pull out a sheet of paper and slide it across his desk to Tucker. "When Brandon submitted his resignation as EMS instructor, he suggested you as his replacement. Of course, before that could happen, you'd have to take courses to get your certification. The hours would be a bit more stable. You'd be off the street and spend more time in a classroom. Not sure if that's a pro or con."

Tucker studied the paper listing educational requirements, salary, outcomes, expectations. He looked at Franco, who leaned on folded arms watching him. "Thank you, sir, for your consideration. I'd like to take some time before giving my answer, if that's okay?"

"Yes, of course, but I will need to know within a week or so."

"You got it, sir. If there's nothing else—"

Before Tucker could finish his sentence, someone rapped on the door before throwing it open. Harrison stood in the doorway. "Excuse the intrusion, sir." His gaze shifted to Tucker. "Dispatch just received a 911 call of a five-year-old male having an allergic reaction to a mushroom. Holland, it's Landon."

Tucker's body went cold.

He forced his rapid-fire pulse to slow as ice slicked his spine. "Let's jump in the truck and go." He pushed past his friend to head for the garage.

Harrison grabbed his arm. "Transport's already been called out. We'll meet him at the hospital."

Tucker rounded back to Franco, his throat thick. "Sir…"

Franco waved him away. "Go, but be careful. That snow's coming down pretty hard and steady now."

Tucker stopped by his desk to grab his cell phone and jacket. He found two missed calls from Willow. For the next ten minutes, he crawled through town behind a snowplow, his wipers working overtime to keep his windshield clear. Even though he wanted nothing more to pass the lumbering vehicle, he needed to stay where he was. The plow was the only way he was able to see where he was going.

Shelby Lake Memorial came into view.
Finally.

He parked quickly, jumped out of his vehicle and raced to the emergency department's automatic doors, the wind whipping though his unzipped jacket.

The dark blue vinyl chairs in the waiting room were full. The wall-mounted TV blared some ridiculous talk show that nobody seemed to be watching.

Tucker darted around a teenage girl feeding a dollar into the vending machine and headed for the triage desk. Christy, one of the emergency department's nurses, looked up from her monitor. "Hey, Tucker. Your son's in bed three." She pressed the button to open the doors to the exam area.

"Thanks." He hurried through the door and located exam room three. He slid open the glass door covered by a blue privacy curtain and found Landon dressed in street clothes lying on the bed, his eyes dark and sunken in his pale face with a nebulizer mask strapped over his nose.

He glanced at Willow, whose eyes were red and blotchy, then hurried to Landon's side, smoothing back his hair and pressing a kiss to his forehead. "Hey, buddy. What's going on?"

Landon pulled the mask away. "I ate a chicken nugget that made me sick."

Tucker looked over at Willow. "A chicken nugget? I thought he ingested a mushroom."

She bit her bottom lip and nodded. "Mom and Dad took us to lunch before they were going to head home. The kids ordered chicken nuggets, and there must have been a leftover breaded mushroom in the fryer, or else one got mixed up in the nuggets somehow. Landon ate half and then said his throat was itchy and bees were in his mouth. I administered his EpiPen and Mom called

911." Tears filled her eyes and spilled down her cheeks. "I'm so sorry, Tucker."

"Hey, it's not your fault. Your quick thinking saved his life." He gave her arm a quick squeeze. "Has he been given Benadryl or steroids yet?"

"Yes, they gave him doses of both and Albuterol to stabilize his breathing. The doctor will be back in a few minutes."

Landon pulled his mask away again. "Daddy, I'm scared."

"Hey, buddy. I'm right here. Don't you worry—the doctors are good. They'll fix you up in no time."

"I don't want a shot."

The desperation in his voice nearly unhinged the emotions had Tucker grappled with while driving through town. Tears warmed his eyes, but he blinked them back. Now wasn't the time to fall apart. His son needed him to be strong.

"I can't promise they won't, Lando, my man. The doctors will do what they think is best, but I will be right beside you the whole time, okay?"

His son nodded, but fear rounded his eyes.

Still holding Landon's hand, Tucker sat on the edge of his son's bed and scanned the vital signs monitor showing Landon's heart rate, blood pressure, oxygen saturation and respiration. He rubbed a thumb and finger over gritty eyes.

The door slid open, and a doctor with dark curly hair wearing scrubs and a white medical jacket entered the room. He extended a hand to Tucker. "I'm Dr. Weller. As you can see, we've administered medicine to open Landon's airways. We've given him Benadryl and started him on a course of steroids. Normally, we'd observe him for three to four hours, but after talking with Landon's pediatrician and getting a family history from your sister-in-law, I think it would be best to keep him overnight to ensure his body reacts positively to the treatments."

Tucker nodded, trying to process the doctor's words.

Christy, one of the nurses, came into the room and assessed Landon's vitals, then turned to Tucker. "They have a room ready for him upstairs. We'll take him up as soon as he's done with this treatment."

The numbers on the monitor screen climbed rapidly as Landon shook his head and tried to pull off the mask, tears leaking down the sides of his face. "No, Daddy. I don't wanna stay. I wanna go home."

Tucker cradled his son's body and pulled him into his lap. Not caring about protocol, he sat on the bed, untangled Landon's monitor wires and held his son against his chest. "Calm down, buddy. I'm not going anywhere. I'll stay with you all night long."

"Promise?"

"Of course."

Feeling his son relax in his arms, Tucker leaned back against the pillow and held him until he fell asleep.

When the orderlies arrived to transport him upstairs, Landon had stirred when Tucker had to release his hold on his son.

Several hours later, after Landon had fallen asleep in the middle of a cartoon, Tucker slipped out of his son's room, leaving the door open.

He stood in front of the window by Landon's room, close enough to sprint back inside if his son awoke.

The snow had stopped, but the storm inside him continued to batter his spirit, leaving him weary and broken.

"Tucker."

He turned to find his dad walking toward him. For a moment, Tucker wished *he* could be the five-year-old once again and run into his father's arms, knowing his dad would make everything better.

Instead, he shoved his hands in his pockets. "Dad. What are you doing here?"

"I came to be with you. So you're not facing the night by yourself."

Tucker's throat thickened as his vision blurred. He scrubbed a hand over his face, struggling for control over his emotions.

He had to think, to figure out how to get through this. To keep his cool and stay strong.

Instead, he wrapped his arms over his chest. "Dad, tell me what to do, how to fix it, how to make the hurt stop. I'm so afraid I'm going to lose him. Like I lost Rayne. Then how will I survive?"

"No matter what you're facing, you're not doing it alone." His voice gruff and thready, Dad opened his arms.

Without a word, Tucker walked into his father's embrace, buried his face in his dad's shoulder and wept.

Chapter Fifteen

Isabella would do just about anything right now to get away. To escape the early snow to a tropical island where she could lie in a hammock under a shady tree while a breeze off the ocean cooled her sun-warmed cheeks. And her biggest decision would be which book to read or dinner to order, what color of flip-flops to wear as she walked along the beach.

But with the temperatures dropping and the late-autumn winds shaking the last clinging leaves from their branches, she was far from a tropical getaway.

She just wanted to clear her head and figure out how to move forward with her tangled life. To forget about her mother's rejection, the guy who'd managed to steal Isabella's heart, the twins who'd burrowed so deeply inside her that she couldn't imagine not being a part of their lives, her father who wanted to sell the diner.

As if she could forget any of them.

And this was why she fought to guard herself and avoid romantic entanglements, because giving away her heart only led to pain.

Her eyes gritty from lack of sleep and tears pressing

for release, she finished cleaning the kitchen at the diner and headed upside to start packing.

Thankfully, Jeanne hadn't found another roommate yet, and since Isabella had paid rent until the end of the month, she'd decided to return to their apartment for the time being until she could figure out what she was going to do with her life.

She'd come back to help Dad move once he decided where he was going, but until then, she needed some distance.

Flipping on the light to her bedroom, she reached for her laptop on her desk. Might as well check for job listings and see what was available.

Her eyes strayed to the framed photo of her and Tucker holding their first-place ribbons in the air after winning the junior cook-off.

Back when life was easy, breezy and carefree.

Or so she'd thought.

Somehow, she needed to pick up the shards of her shattered heart and piece them back together.

Cradling her laptop against her chest, Isabella slid onto her bed and pressed her back against the headboard. She kicked off her shoes and dug her toes under the knitted afghan at the end of her bed.

"You look like you're fifteen all over again."

Isabella looked up to find her dad standing in the doorway with one shoulder pressed against the doorjamb. "Mind if I come in?"

She waved him in and set her closed laptop on her nightstand.

"How are you doing?"

She shrugged. "Fine. Figured I'd see what jobs were available, then I'll start packing."

"Why?"

"You've been so surly since you came home from the hospital. I feel like I've been a major inconvenience since I've been here, but don't worry, I'm leaving in the morning and moving back in with Jeanne. I'll be out of your way so you can do whatever you want with the diner. I'll take as much of my stuff as will fit in my car and make arrangements to have the rest donated."

"If you're moving back in with Jeanne, does that mean you took Justin up on his job offer?"

"No way. Justin's a jerk, and I never want to work anywhere near him again. He said I was a greasy spoon girl and that's all I'll ever be. Maybe he's right. I don't know. I'm not even sure I really care. And after his snide comments at the competition, it's apparent he never believed in my abilities. I'm moving back in with Jeanne because I need a place to sleep while I figure out what to do next."

"Oh man. Bells, I messed up. Big-time." Dad scraped a hand over his face then moved closer to sit on the corner of her bed. "I have a confession—I lied about wanting to sell the diner."

She stared at him, struggling with wanting to hug him and wanting to wring his neck. "Why would you do that?"

"I overheard your conversation with Justin and didn't want the diner to stand in the way of your career."

"What is it with you men jumping to conclusions and deciding what you feel is best for me? I'm a grown woman who can make her own choices, you know?"

He nodded. "Yes, I do know. But being your old dad, I just want what's best for you."

"Even if it means pushing me away? Like Mom?"

"I'm nothing like her and you know it."

"Sorry, cheap shot."

Red crawled up his neck. "I'm sorry—that's the last thing I wanted to do."

"So, what's going on?"

Dad pushed off the bed and walked to her window. He crossed his arms over his chest. "I saw your mother."

Isabella blinked and shook her head as if someone had thrown a bucket of ice water in her face. "What? What do you mean you saw my mother? At the competition? Did you talk to her?"

He shook his head. "No, this was several months ago—at the beginning of her tour to promote her new cookbook. I drove to Pittsburgh, bought her book, stood in line for two hours to have her sign it, rehearsing my words over and over, only to have her not recognize me. Even when I asked her to sign the book to my daughter, Isabella. Not one flinch, no comment about her daughter being named the same. Nothing."

Isabella moved off the bed and walked over to him, pressing a hand to his back. "Oh Dad…"

He shoved his hands in his front pockets and shrugged. "I just didn't care about much. I wasn't feeling well. Went to the doctor and learned about the diabetes, but I didn't even care about watching my diet or anything. Started picking fights with George. Business was sliding. I needed new equipment, so I got a loan, but then I didn't care about paying it back. And now it may be too late."

"No, it's not. We aren't giving up."

"Bells, you've always been an encourager, quick to see the good in people and wanting the best for me. But let's face it—my irresponsibility has caused this. Maybe it *would* be best to sell the diner. People are complaining about the changes anyway."

Changes she'd forced on him.

"So what? We can't please everyone, Dad. Focus on

doing what's good and right for the diner. George was a grumpy old man who didn't respect you. Get someone younger in here who has a passion for cooking and wants to learn from one of the best. If we have to close down again to retrain a whole new staff, then so be it."

He heaved a sigh and shook his head. "No, Bells. I can't. I'm too tired to do this alone."

"Who said you were doing it alone? I'm by your side— the same place I've been since you bought this diner."

"I thought you were moving back in with Jeanne."

"Only because I felt like you were pushing me away."

"I'm sorry. I guess I couldn't get out of my own way. You came in so ready to revive a failing diner, and I felt like you didn't need me, so I tucked tail and stayed away. Then Tucker approached me about working with his family on the community garden. I should've been more appreciative. Instead I pushed you all away. Can you forgive me?"

Tears filled her eyes. "Of course. But Dad, I will always need you. You have the expertise and know customers like Bernie who wants a spoonful of chicken broth over his eggs, but you need to evolve instead of being stuck in a time warp. And you need some healthy options to balance the greasy spoon fare."

He reached for her chin. "And you need to be yourself—you're a fantastic cook, especially with your homemade comfort foods that people were raving about when the diner reopened. Chef Scott was correct—you know how to take the ordinary and make it extraordinary. But Joe's All-Star Diner is not a fine-dining establishment."

"Well, maybe I can do a little of both worlds."

"What do you mean?"

She explained about catering Jake and Tori's wedding and the requests that came from that event. "I love doing those events, and I need a licensed kitchen, so what if we partner? I will help out with the diner when needed and work on expanding my catering business. And you will stop keeping me in the dark about stuff."

He wrapped his strong, muscular arms around her and rested his chin on the top of her head. "Now that's a partnership I think I can work with. How about we create a business plan and then talk to the bank together? Even though the past few months have been a bit patchy, I'm sure they'll give you a start-up loan, especially if I cosign for you."

"Dad, you've done so much for me already. Let's get the diner squared away, and then we can focus on expanding. Oh, and if that man wasn't interested in buying the diner, then who was he?"

"Leonard's my new accountant. Realizing I can't do it all, I decided to give up jobs that I detest, like accounting and payroll."

She shook her head. "You deceived me."

"And I'm sorry. Let me ask—how does Tucker fit into your plans?"

"Tucker? He's just a friend. There's no future for us."

"Don't be so sure. I've seen the way he's looked at you, and honestly, that man has more than friendship on his mind."

As much as Isabella wanted to lean into her father's words and let them take hold, it was much safer to believe she and Tucker were destined for nothing more than friendship. That way, maybe she could work at putting her heart back together, piece by piece.

What had he done?

Tucker sat in an uncomfortable chair next to Landon's bed while his son slept, fatigued from the allergic reaction that nearly wrecked his small body. Bracing his elbows on his knees, he cradled his head in his hands.

Still dressed in his paramedic uniform from yesterday and a day's worth of shadow scruffing his jaw, Tucker longed for a hot shower and his own bed.

The last forty-eight hours have filled him a raw weariness he couldn't seem to shake. Last night, he'd tried to doze next to Landon's bed, but every sound and movement had him shooting to his feet for fear of losing his son.

And if that wasn't stressful enough, he couldn't get Bella out of his thoughts.

The last thing he wanted was to keep her from pursuing her career.

But apparently he wasn't enough.

Landon's day nurse came into the room, her soles quiet against the gleaming tile. She checked Landon's oxygen stats and the rest of his vitals and made notations on the laptop she carried. She smiled at Tucker. "If you want to grab some coffee or something, I can sit with him for a bit, so if he wakes up, he won't be alone and scared."

Nodding, Tucker scrubbed a hand over his face and stood. He needed coffee. Something to revive his brain cells that continued to scatter his thoughts.

Then maybe he could swing by the gift shop and buy a T-shirt and a razor to help him feel a little more human.

He rode the elevator to the first floor. The doors opened to reveal his family standing on the other side waiting to get on—Dad, Claudia, Jake, Tori and even Evan and Micah. And Olivia.

"Daddy!" Livie barreled into him, wrapping her arms around his legs.

He stepped off the elevator and scooped her up and crushed her to him, her presence filling in some of the cracks and crevices in his chest. "What are you doing here? Did you drive?"

"Daddy, you're so silly. Papa drove us." Livie shimmied out of his arms and raced over to grab Micah's left hand. "Look, Uncle Micah's here, too."

"I see that." His chest swelled as he connected gazes with each of his brothers. Jake, dressed in his faded jeans and an untucked flannel shirt standing at parade rest. Evan, face still tanned in mid-November with sun-highlighted short hair, wore a long-sleeved T-shirt advertising a kayaking company and olive-green cargo shorts with a pair of leather flip-flops. Micah, his full beard nearly concealing the red, puckered skin on the right side of his face, had long, shaggy hair and wore a faded sweatshirt with the right sleeve hanging empty at his side, jeans with holes in the knees and worn, unlaced combat boots.

Tucker pushed through the lump forming in his throat and forced a smile in place. "What are you guys doing here?"

The brothers exchanged glances, then Evan shrugged. "Dad called, so we came. We're here for you, dude."

Jake pulled Tucker into a quick hug and clapped him on the back. "We're Holland strong, remember? We may bend, but we don't break, right?"

He wasn't so sure about the not breaking part…he was pretty sure a part of him had been broken beyond repair. But he forced a smile. "How many times did Dad have you guys repeating that on the way down?"

"However many times it takes for you knuckleheads to remember it." Dad clapped a hand on Tucker's shoulder and gave it a gentle squeeze. "How are you doing?"

If anyone else had asked that same question, Tucker would've faked it with a shrug and a "fine." But his dad had the superpower of being able to zero in on the truth.

Tucker fisted his hands in the front pockets of his black cargo pants. He dropped his chin to his chest, then slowly shook his head as tears filled his eyes. His chest shuddered, and he clamped down on his bottom lip. Maybe the pain in his mouth would take away from the destruction in his chest.

Landon was going to be fine. The doctor had assured him of that several times, but seeing his son lie on the bed fighting for breath…that had dredged up memories best forgotten, and he wasn't sure how to move forward.

Dad looped an arm around his shoulder. "Come on. Let's take a walk."

"Can't. I need to get back to Landon."

"Claudia and Tori can sit with him for a few minutes."

They paused at a coffee cart in the lobby for two cups of strong coffee, then moved down the hall. Dad opened a door and stepped aside for Tucker to enter the room marked *Chapel.*

Two sections of about twenty chairs faced a narrow pulpit flanked by stained glass. Low lighting and soft instrumental hymns created a reverent atmosphere.

Tucker slid into the last row and sat on one of the padded chairs.

"So, what's going on?"

Tucker took a sip of his coffee, then set it on the floor next to his feet. He cupped his mouth and blew out a breath. Dropping his hands between his knees, he glanced at Dad then focused on the threads in the scarlet-colored carpet. "Between Bella and Landon, I'm not sure how much more I can take."

"You're strong. Stronger than you think." Dad removed the lid of his coffee and took a sip. "Good coffee. You're a rescuer, Tuck—the first to jump in, save the day and bail others out of trouble, which is why Evan and Micah turn to you first for help. Keeping your cool is your superpower."

"I'm not doing such a good job of that right now. It's been tough being the strong one all the time. It's my job, but I'm failing. Even though Landon will make a full recovery, I can't shake this helpless feeling."

"Disaster tends to shake your core, and son, you've had your share of disasters the past few years. I gotta say I'm surprised you've been able to keep it together as well as you have. So why do you think you need to be the strong one all the time?"

"Remember the day I turned ten and Mom had that miscarriage?"

"Yep. That was a tough day for her. For all of us."

"You told me it was my job to stay strong."

"You did stay strong. You called 911. You saved Mom's life even though she'd lost the baby." Dad rubbed a hand over his forehead. "I'm sorry if I made you feel you always had to be strong."

"When I arrived at the hospital yesterday and saw Landon on that stretcher, I felt everything within me was crumbling and I was going to lose him the same way I'd lost Rayne. I just can't shake this sense of panic. There's nothing I can do for him, and I feel so helpless." Tucker's chest shuddered as his eyes filled.

"Tucker, you're a fine paramedic, but you are not God. It's not your job to save everyone. Sometimes, your job is to just trust God to show up."

"What if He doesn't? Like when Mom was killed? Or when Rayne died?"

"Oh, son. He was there." Chuck thumped Tucker's chest. "Right here. You just need to keep trusting Him no matter the outcome. No matter what life throws at us, He keeps holding on, never letting go. When we continue to find hope in the heartache, that's what draws us closer to Him."

"That's what Mom used to tell us, too."

"She was a smart woman. When feed prices dropped, milk prices rose or one of you boys was sick, she'd always remind me, 'You have two choices, Chuck—trust God or go it alone. You can't claim to be a Christian and lack faith. Let your faith be greater than your fear. Stop listening to the enemy's voice and tune in to God's.'"

Tucker smiled genuinely for the first time in a couple of days. "I can hear her saying that. Man, I miss her."

"Me, too. As I've said before—I'll always love your mother. Her death doesn't change that. Just as I suspect you'll always love Rayne. I remember the day we learned Lilly was pregnant with you, and she asked what was eating at me. I confessed that I loved Jacob so much that I didn't know if I could love another child. She said the amazing thing about the heart is it grows with more and more opportunities to love. The more we exercise it, the bigger it gets. Grieving your mother was the hardest thing I've ever had to do, but I kept trusting God. After Dennis died and Claudia and I grew closer, God tapped me on the shoulder and said she was to be my new wife."

"I didn't handle things well with Bella."

"It's not too late to change that. Talk to her. Tell her how you feel."

"What if she doesn't want me? Then what? I'm supposed to just walk away?"

"You're both worn-out and running on empty. Let God fill you up."

"I'm scared."

"And that's okay. Just make sure your faith is stronger than your fear. Faith and trust go hand in hand, and it's a choice you need to make every single day, even several times a day. So now it's up to you to decide if you're willing to fight for what you want. You're a strong, brave man, but you can't go into battle alone." Dad stood and stretched his back. "Once Landon's ready to go home, Claudia and I will come down and stay with him, so you can find Isabella and share your heart."

They headed out into the hall to find Jake sitting on the bench outside the chapel.

"What are you doing here?"

Jake pushed to his feet. "Dad's right, you know."

Tucker scrubbed a hand over the back of his head. "Of course, but what in particular?"

"If you'd told me six months ago Tori and I would be remarried before the end of the year, I probably would've decked you." Jake slugged him playfully on the shoulder, then held up his left hand, sporting a shiny new wedding ring. "But now, look how far we've come. Now it's my turn to tell you, fight for what you want, because when you find that person who gets you—faults and all—then you need to hold on tight. We've been dealt heartaches that brought us to our knees, but like you told me over the summer when I was wrestling over what to do about Tori—God's offering you a second chance. It's time to close the door to the past and open the one to a future with Isabella."

Tucker pulled his brother in for a hug and thumped him on the back. "Thanks, brother."

He followed Jake to the elevator and pressed the button for Landon's floor to see if the doctor was willing to discharge him yet.

Once his son was stable and settled, Tucker was going to find the courage to go after Bella, even if he had to drive back to New York to find her.

He didn't know what he was going to say, but he was

willing to fight for the woman he loved and give her the life she deserved.

Even if she didn't realize it yet.

Chapter Sixteen

Tucker Holland had some explaining to do. And Isabella wanted answers.

She marched up Tucker's walk, pressed the doorbell three times and pounded on the door. "Tucker! Open up!"

Barking sounded from inside the house.

A moment later, the door flew open and Tucker stood in the doorway wearing gray sweatpants, a red Shelby Lake Lions T-shirt and bare feet. His hair looked like he'd hurriedly combed it with a garden rake.

Meno and Dory dashed out the door, jumping up on her legs.

Seeing his bleary eyes, remorse hit her. "I woke you. I'm sorry. Go back to bed. We'll talk later." She turned and headed down the steps.

"Oh no, you don't." He reached out and grabbed her arm before she could get too far. "You don't get to wake me up from a sound sleep and then walk away."

Isabella turned slowly and looked at him as heat scalded her cheeks. "I'm really sorry about that. I wasn't thinking."

Tucker dragged a hand through his hair. "How about

if you come inside and tell me what has you in such an uproar?"

He held the door open and moved aside so she could pass. The dogs charged ahead of her and danced in circles as she stepped into his house. She forced herself not to think about the last time she'd visited and left.

Opening her purse, she pulled out a letter and thrust it at him. "Care to tell me what this is all about?"

He took the envelope but didn't move to open it. He tapped it against his palm. "I paid off your dad's loan."

"Why?"

Tucker tossed the letter on the side table by the door. "Talk to your dad."

"I tried. He said I needed to talk to you. Would someone tell me what's going on?"

Tucker dragged a hand through his hair. "Did you know Landon was rushed to the hospital?"

Isabella's eyes widened. "No, what happened?"

Now she felt even worse for waking him up.

"An allergic reaction." He shared about Landon eating the deep fried mushroom. "Willow acted quickly, but they called 911 just in case, especially after what had happened with Rayne."

"You must've been terrified."

"Something like that. While we were at the hospital, I talked with my dad. I gotta admit, I was a bit of a mess—not my best moment."

"You don't have to be the strong one all the time. Is Landon okay now?"

"Yes, after they kept him overnight for observation, he's perfectly fine. Anyway, Dad shared some necessary truth with me. After we left the chapel, Jake reminded me God had given me a second chance and I'd be a fool to let it go. I wanted to do something to show you how serious I was about wanting to partner with you, so I went to the diner and had a long talk with Joe, including how I felt about you. I wanted to know what I could do to win you back."

"What did he say?"

"He mentioned your desire to start a catering business through the restaurant and said you were holding off because you wanted to help pay off his loan before you accrued more debt. Then I knew what I needed to do to show you I was serious about wanting to be your partner."

Tears pricked her eyes as she gazed at the letter on the table.

No one had offered such a grand gesture before. "Oh, Tucker. I'm..." She sighed, her hand pressed against her chest. "It's so kind and generous, but it's too much. I can't pay you back for quite a while."

He sandwiched her hands between his. "Bella, this is a gift. One given with no strings and no conditions."

"But what about Livie and Landon? That money needs to go to them."

"I saved their mother's life insurance money for their futures. I've been saving money earned through the reserves. I promise you—no one is going without because I did this."

"Why would you do this for me?"

"Isn't it obvious?"

"I'm feeling a little obtuse these days, so how about you spell it out for me?"

He took a step toward her and cupped her face in his hands, his blueberry-colored eyes tangling with hers. A slow smile spread across his face. "Because I love you."

Her heart stilled.

He spoke so softly and so gently that she must have misheard him.

Her eyes searched his. "No, you can't love me. You love Rayne. There's no room in your heart for me."

He frowned, lowered his hands and took a step back. "Why would you think that?"

"Because that day during the Dinner with a Hero fundraiser, you said you had your happily-ever-after already and you weren't looking to fall in love again."

Even saying the words aloud—words she'd repeated over and over in her heart—created an ache in her chest.

"And if I recall, you said falling in love only led to heartbreak. At that time, I had no intention of falling in love. With what I'd had with my late wife, I didn't think I could find that again. But I was wrong."

Tucker led her into the living room. He scooped up several stuffed animals and dumped them over the back of the sectional. He patted the couch for Isabella to sit.

She sat on the edge of the cushion, and Dory pawed at her leg to be picked up. She held the pregnant rescue dog in her lap and faced Tucker as he sat beside her. "What changed?"

His eyes softened as he brushed a finger along her jaw. "You."

Her hand flew to her chest. "Me? What did I do?"

"From the time we were teenagers, you respected my relationship with my wife. And since we agreed to partner up, you've taken awesome care of my kids. The way you were willing to sacrifice your goals and dreams to help your dad…well, the more I was around you, the more I hated to leave you."

"But we're just friends."

"Bella, I'm grateful for your friendship." He reached for her hands. "But let's face it. Since I've been spending more and more time with you, you haven't been just a friend. Despite arguing with myself about it, I realized I wanted more than friendship from you. I come with rambunctious five-year-olds and a couple of dogs, one of which is going to have puppies soon. However, I will do whatever it takes and go wherever you want to go to be with you."

She laughed as tears warmed her eyes. "Sounds like a perfect combination. I will never try to take Rayne's place in their lives, but I will continue to love Livie and Landon as if they were my own. I came home as a hungry chef—not for food, but for connection and fulfillment of who I wanted to be. And you and your family gave that to me. I would love to go back to helping you care for Livie and Landon, but I don't want to get in the way of Willow's time with them."

"Actually, my schedule may be changing." Tucker told her about EMS instructor opportunity. "With everything that happened with Landon, I haven't had time to process it. I need to pray and ask for God's leading about my career and if continuing to pursue my counseling degree is the way to go."

"Whatever you decide, you won't have to face anything alone. I'm here to support you every step of the way."

"My mom used to say the more you exercise your heart, the more it grows, giving you more opportunities for loving others." Tucker pressed his palms against hers, then twined his fingers around hers. "I'm not gonna lie, Bella. I will always love Rayne. She was a great wife and a wonderful mother, and she's a part of my past. But you were wrong—there is room in my heart for you. If you'll have us, we want you to be a part of our present and, hopefully, our future."

"I just didn't want to be her stand-in."

"You were never that. You've been the lead in your

own story for a very long time. Now you just need the courage to live it. It's your turn to be the star and stand out with the gifts God has given you."

"And you're the dashing hero who rescued me."

"You've got that all wrong—you're the one who rescued me. With a two-hundred-dollar picnic basket. You resuscitated my heart and helped it to start beating again. I love you, Isabella Bradley, and I'm excited to see what plans God has in store for us."

Isabella listened to his heart beating strong and steady against her ear. "I love you, too, Tucker Holland. I think I've loved you for the last fifteen years."

"Say it again. I'll never get tired of hearing it." He drew her into the cradle of his embrace and brushed a kiss across her lips.

Epilogue

Fingers of sunlight parted the canopy of leaves shading her booth at the farmers market as the midmorning breeze sashayed across Isabella's face, tangoing with the hairs that strayed from her French twist.

Content.

That's how she felt about her life these days.

Heavy boxes sat in the beds and on tailgates of pickup trunks while vendors loaded baskets of assorted sizes with fresh fruits and vegetables. A gardener across the path from Isabella's booth displayed cut flowers in mason jars, the blooms fragrancing the air. Behind him, kayakers floated down the river, which glistened like silver.

Children ran down the dirt path to the playground as their parents, pushing strollers, tried to keep up with them.

A sudden gust of wind stirred the display on the booth Isabella shared with her father and the Holland Family Farm's community garden. She rescued the light blue beverage napkins and righted them next to the pamphlets and business cards promoting her new business—Bella Joe's Catering.

She retied the strings to her blue-and-white-pinstriped

apron worn over a scoop-neck white T-shirt and black pants. With the July temperatures climbing even before noon, she'd shed her chef jacket to avoid heatstroke.

While people stopped by the U-shaped booth to chat with her father, who seemed to know everyone in the community, he introduced them to Jonah and Vanessa Healy, the first family to enroll in the Fatigues to Farming program. They'd been helping him with the community garden, which had had a successful first run, based on the amount of produce on the table.

Jonah, who'd lost his leg overseas while on embassy duty, chatted with Dad about canning tomatoes. Jonah's wife, Vanessa, bagged zucchini for a customer.

Isabella pulled out a container of raspberry profiteroles with Chantilly cream and chocolate ganache and refilled her sampler tray. Of course, they weren't as fresh as they had been when made this morning, but hopefully they would draw those interested in her catering services.

Although since Jake and Tori Holland's wedding and Tucker's generous investment, her calendar was filling with events faster than she had anticipated.

Yep, life was good.

The past eight months with Tucker, Livie and Landon had been better than she could have imagined.

"Izzie!"

At the sound of her name, Isabella turned, and a smile spread across her face.

She rounded the booth and held her arms out wide. Livie, dressed in a white T-shirt with a purple heart and a matching ruffled skirt, flew into her arms. Her high ponytail tickled Isabella's nose. "Hey, punkin, what are you doing here? Did you drive Daddy's car without him?"

"Oh, Izzie. You're silly. I came with Daddy." She

pointed over her shoulder at Tucker about four feet behind. He held a dual leash with Meno and Dory in the lead.

At the sight of him, Isabella's heart tumbled against her ribs.

He wore a long-sleeved button-down shirt cuffed to his elbows, exposing tanned muscular forearms. With his khaki shorts, he could have walked off the pages of an Eddie Bauer catalog.

To her, he looked perfect.

Behind him, Landon bounced between Chuck and Claudia, chattering about something.

Jake and Tori, hand in hand, paused at the Bee's Knees booth. He wrapped a protective arm over her five-month baby bump while she sampled clover honey.

"Hey, you." Tucker's velvety voice dipped low, and he feathered a kiss across Isabella's mouth.

"Hey, yourself." She clasped her hands behind her back to keep from twining them around his neck and twirling her fingers in the curls at his nape.

"Got a minute?"

"For you, I have two."

His lips tipped up as he placed his hands on her shoulders. Then he slid them slowly down her arms until he detached her hands from behind her back and slid his fingers between hers. "Bella…"

He paused as he lifted his blue eyes. The playfulness left only to be replaced with the same gentle expression he wore every time he told her he loved her.

He wore that expression often.

And each time her heart stilled as she tried to remind herself that was her new reality.

"Bella, the moment I walked across the farmers market last fall when we had our first date, I knew I was walking toward my future. You know from hanging out with us these last eight months, my life is chaotic at times with active twins and more dogs than one family needs, but I'm crazy about you, so we want to ask you something." Releasing her hand, he nodded to Landon and Livie.

Landon grabbed Livie's hand. "Come on, Livie."

They stood in front of Isabella holding something behind their backs, took deep breaths, then spoke in loud unison. "Izzie, we love you."

She knelt in front of them. "I love you, too."

"We gotta ask you something."

Her heart leaped. Not trusting her voice, she bit her lower lip and nodded.

They pulled cards out from behind their backs. Her eyes widened as she read the words.

Will You Marry Us?

Childish scrawl and drawn hearts and flowers released a flood of tears that trickled down her cheeks.

Tucker pulled a small box from his front pocket and opened it to reveal a diamond solitaire.

A sob shuddered in her chest.

"Why are you crying? This is happy stuff." Landon gave her an eye roll and batted at the ground with his card. "Man, girls are so 'motional."

She gathered the twins in her arms and kissed their cheeks. "These are happy tears, you goof."

Landon wriggled out of her arms and scrubbed a hand across his cheek. "Gross."

Laughter bubbled in her throat. She released Livie, then turned to Tucker, who lowered to one knee in front of her. "Isabella Bradley, I can't promise our lives won't be chaotic, but I promise no one will love you more than I do, and I want to spend the rest of our lives showing you just how much. Will you marry us?"

"Tucker Holland, I love you. We both know how hard life can be. I will marry you. The whole crazy, chaotic, beautiful package."

The gathered crowd clapped and whistled, but she ignored them. Pulling Tucker to his feet, she cupped his face in her hands. "I've been waiting my whole life for you."

"Yay!" Livie clapped her hands. "I'm so 'cited. Izzie's going to be our new mommy."

Mommy.

Her heart sang over the beauty of that name.

He pressed his forehead against hers. Capturing her hand, he slid the ring on her finger, cradled it against his chest. Then he wrapped her in the security of his embrace and spoke into her ear. "Before you walked back into my life, I was imprisoned in my grief, but you freed me, giving me the greatest gift—a second chance at happily-ever-after."

Lowering his head, he kissed her breathless, sealing his words.

After being held captive to the fear that love only led to heartbreak, Tucker's promise offered her what she needed most—a love redeemed.

* * * * *

If you loved this story,
pick up Love Inspired author Lisa Jordan's
previous books set in Shelby Lake

Lakeside Sweethearts
Lakeside Redemption
Lakeside Romance
Season of Hope

Available now from Love Inspired!

Find more great reads at LoveInspired.com

Dear Reader,

When I introduced Tucker in *Season of Hope*, I knew he was someone who hid a lot of his pain but he continued to push forward to be there for others. His motto was "just keep swimming."

When Tucker married Rayne, they expected to grow old together. But after a decade, their happily ever after had been cut short by tragedy. And suddenly Tucker was a single father.

Grief comes in many forms—death of a loved one, death of a relationship, death of a dream. It's like a powerful fist that punches you in the chest, stealing your breath and makes you wonder how you will ever survive.

But through time, prayer, counsel and encouragement from those who have walked that road, you move through it, treasuring those memories you've created. And those memory triggers start to bring smiles instead of tears. Through it all, though, when we keep our eyes on God and our hand in His, He will guide us and fill in those cracked, broken places with His grace and mercy.

Friends, just know you are not alone. God is with you every step of the way. He feels your pain. And that pain won't be wasted. It can draw you closer to Him if you allow it. In the midst of the darkness, He shines His light. He has a plan and purpose for your life and He wants you to call out to Him and seek Him with your whole heart.

Thank you for reading Tucker and Isabella's story. I love to hear from my readers. Visit me at www.lisajordanbooks.com and email me at lisa@lisajordanbooks.com.

All my heart,
Lisa Jordan

WE HOPE YOU ENJOYED
THIS BOOK FROM

LOVE INSPIRED
INSPIRATIONAL ROMANCE

Uplifting stories of faith, forgiveness and hope.

Fall in love with stories where faith helps
guide you through life's challenges, and discover
the promise of a new beginning.

6 NEW BOOKS AVAILABLE EVERY MONTH!

COMING NEXT MONTH FROM
Love Inspired

Available September 15, 2020

THE AMISH CHRISTMAS SECRET
Indiana Amish Brides • by Vannetta Chapman

Becca Schwartz is positive something's off with her next-door neighbor. Why would Daniel Glick move to the only farm worse than her family's if he can afford an exquisite new horse? Her focus must stay on her family's desperate financial straits. But as she falls for Daniel, his secret could change her life forever...

THE AMISH WIDOW'S CHRISTMAS HOPE
Amish of Serenity Ridge • by Carrie Lighte

When single mother Fern Glick inherits her uncle's home at Christmastime, she has no intention of living in the same town as widower Walker Huyard—her ex-fiancé who left her to marry her cousin. But can he convince her to stay without breaking his promise to never reveal certain details of the past?

THE COWBOY'S CHRISTMAS BLESSINGS
Wyoming Sweethearts • by Jill Kemerer

Offering a cabin to a friend in need and her triplet babies for the holidays is an easy decision for rancher Judd Wilson. But when Nicole Taylor insists on helping him build a gingerbread house for his aunt to return the favor, can he avoid losing his heart to the single mother?

FINDING HER CHRISTMAS FAMILY
Golden Grove • by Ruth Logan Herne

Only one thing stands between Sarah and her late sister's daughters this Christmas: Renzo Calloway, their deputy sheriff guardian. Sarah never even knew her sister existed until recently, and Renzo is the only family her nieces know. Together, can they build a future that includes the girls...and each other?

ALASKAN CHRISTMAS REDEMPTION
Home to Owl Creek • by Belle Calhoune

Struggling to keep her diner afloat through the holidays, Piper Miller turns to her best friend, Braden North, for help. But as they work together to find ways to revitalize her business, Braden must keep the truth about a tragedy from their past hidden...or risk losing Piper for good.

UNEXPECTED CHRISTMAS JOY
by Gabrielle Meyer

Actress Kate LeClair doesn't know the first thing about babies, yet she's just become the guardian of eighteen-month-old triplets. Asking experienced single father Pastor Jacob Dawson for help with the little boys might just give Kate the greatest Christmas gift of all—family.

LOVE INSPIRED

INSPIRATIONAL ROMANCE

IS LOOKING FOR NEW AUTHORS!

Do you have an idea for an inspirational
contemporary romance book?

Do you enjoy writing faith-based romances about small-town
men and women who overcome challenges and fall in love?

We're looking for new authors for Love Inspired,
and we want to see your story!

Check out our writing guidelines and
submit your Love Inspired manuscript at
Harlequin.com/Submit

CONNECT WITH US AT:

www.LoveInspired.com

Facebook.com/LoveInspiredBooks

Twitter.com/LoveInspiredBks

Facebook.com/groups/HarlequinConnection